DARK MINDS
PRESS

RUIN

Published by
Dark Minds Press
31 Gristmill Close
Cheltenham
Glos.
GL51 0PZ
www.darkmindspress.com
Mail@darkmindspress.com
First Print Edition – October 2016
Cover Image © 77studios
www.77studios.blogspot.com

Interior layout by Anthony Watson

ISBN-13: 978-1535229265
ISBN-10: 1535229268

DARK MINDS
NOVELLAS

4

RUIN

A novella

by

Rich Hawkins

PROLOGUE

It was sixty days since the black rocks fell in screaming fire from the sky. Fifty days since the blight appeared upon trees and other flora. Forty days since vast numbers of livestock became sick and had to be destroyed.

Soon after that, the virus jumped to its first human host and began to spread through the population.

The south of England was infected.

*

Gus Abernathy watched steam rise from the tomato soup warming on the hob. The kitchen lights flickered. He looked up at the ceiling and hoped it wasn't the prelude to another blackout, because he was down to the last few candles and the local supermarket had sold out during the week. He had ordered some on the internet, but he wasn't expecting them through the post anytime soon. Even Royal Mail had stopped delivering last week, after several of their drivers were killed at blockades near Southampton.

The portable radio on the worktop told of more protests and demonstrations in London. The newscaster's voice was barely audible above the hiss of static. Gus tried to tune in the radio, but couldn't get a good signal, and when the soup began to bubble and spit he gave up and lifted the pot from the cooker and poured it into a small bowl. He placed the bowl and a buttered slice of bread on a plastic tray. A glass of water completed the meagre meal.

With the harsh light of the kitchen behind him, Gus climbed the stairs while trying to keep the tray level and not spill any soup or water. Thin carpet under his feet and old walls to his flanks. Creaking pipes in unseen places. The sound of the radio faded as he reached the landing. He walked to Tom's bedroom and pushed the door open with one elbow and stepped into the stink of illness and fever-sweat. It was a struggle not to cringe and grimace at the stale thickness of the air.

The soft glow of the lamp revealed the thin, pale boy in the small bed. Eyes closed, face turned to the ceiling, shivering beneath the *Spider-Man* duvet that covered him to the neck and smelled of unwashed skin. Dark hair was plastered to his clammy forehead, where prominent veins pulsed under the skin. Lips dried out and painfully cracked, sore and red at the corners of his mouth.

Gus sat on the chair at the bedside. Posters of footballers adorned the walls: Messi, Ronaldo, Neymar, and Harry Kane. The Premier League and all the other leagues below were cancelled for the foreseeable future. Various sports events had gone the same way.

Gus looked at the boy and cleared his throat.

Tom opened his red-rimmed eyes. The skin around them looked tender and puffy, darkened from exhaustion. He turned his face towards Gus. The glazed dampness within them caused a wince in Gus's heart.

"I brought you some dinner," Gus said. He tried to smile, but it was beyond him.

Tom's voice was nothing more than a stifled whisper. "I'm not hungry, Dad."

"You have to eat something, to keep your strength up."

Tom shook his head.

"You sure? It's my special recipe soup."

"It's from a tin, Dad."

"I still had to warm it up on the hob."

"No thanks, Dad."

"Okay." Gus placed the tray on the floor. "Do you want some water?"

Tom nodded once. His eyes fluttered.

Gus leaned closer to Tom and carefully tipped the glass to the boy's lips. Tom's throat worked as he swallowed. He spluttered droplets from his mouth. Gus withdrew the glass then took a tissue and dabbed at Tom's chin. When the boy pulled his arms from underneath the duvet, the hands at the end of them were trembling and almost useless.

Gus offered more water, but Tom declined, staring at the ceiling as the breath rattled from his thin chest. Gus watched him in silence, trying to conjure comforting words for the boy, but he couldn't, so he just sat there with the glass of water in his hands, feeling as useless and impotent as he'd ever done.

With his eyes still fixed on the ceiling, Tom said, "I don't think I'll be going to school tomorrow."

"That's okay," said Gus. "I think school's cancelled. Indefinitely."

"Some of my teachers got sick. So did some of my classmates. I think they're all dead by now."

Gus didn't answer. He was wringing his hands.

"I dreamed of Mum earlier," Tom said.

"You did?"

"She was happy."

"That's good."

"I miss her."

"Same here," Gus said. "Miss her every day."

Tom looked at him. "I'm glad she never got to see me like this."

"Don't talk like that."

The boy coughed wetly and wiped his mouth. "It's true. I know what's gonna happen to me."

"You're going to be fine."

"Before I got ill, I saw what the people on the telly said. No one recovers. No one gets better. They said that if you catch it, you die."

"They weren't certain," Gus muttered. "Nothing's certain."

"It's okay, Dad." A wan smile appeared on Tom's face; something like acceptance from a boy who'd barely lived a fragment of a life. It broke Gus's heart and made him hopeless.

Tears welled in his eyes as he regarded his son. "I'll never leave you, my boy."

"I know, Dad. I know."

Shoulders sagging with worry and sadness, Gus imagined the diseased air being pulled into his lungs as he breathed in. He'd seen how easily the blight had spread, and knew that if he was infected it was already too late for him. If the virus was propagating in his blood, he was no more than a dead man waiting to die. In the last week, each night before bed, he'd stood before the bathroom mirror and checked his skin and eyes for the tell-tale signs of the blight, and each night he'd found nothing.

And a small part of him was angered by this, because his only comfort was the hope that he'd die in the same house as his son. They would die together and that would be that.

Tom's voice woke him from his thoughts.

"Someone's coming."

"What?"

"To take me away, Dad…"

Gus heard a vehicle pull up outside. A large engine idled in the street, mixing with indistinct voices and garbled radio chatter. Gus went to the window and peered between the curtains. The powerful headlights of an army truck reflected on the damp road. Soldiers in gas masks held rifles as they disembarked from the back of the truck. Gus watched as several of the soldiers crossed the street to Mike Potter's house and started banging on the front door. After a few moments, when there was no answer, they kicked the door down and rushed inside as muffled shouts and cries came from beyond the doorway. Someone screamed – it sounded like Mike's wife – and then there was a single gunshot and it all went silent.

Seconds later, Mike was dragged crying from the house and hauled onto the truck.

Gus retreated from the window, his hands to his mouth.

"Are they going to take me, Dad?" Tom asked.

Before Gus could answer, the soldiers were knocking on the front door, demanding to be let in. He went to his son and sat at the bedside.

"It'll be okay, Tom. We'll sort this out. It's probably just a misunderstanding."

The soldiers fell silent at the door, a moment in which Gus listened to his heartbeat flail inside his skull. Tom whimpered and asked questions Gus couldn't answer.

Gus flinched at the crash of the front door being smashed open. Indistinct shouts. Feet trampling up the stairs.

It was all inevitable, he supposed. This was the way of things now.

When the door opened, Gus stood and turned to the soldiers faceless behind their gas masks. He flinched from the torchlights fixed upon their rifles; he held his ground when they were directed towards his face and raised his hands in a supplicating gesture, but the soldiers pushed him aside and pulled Tom from the bed.

Gus reached for his son, but when something hard hit him square in the face, his legs crumpled and he fell down next to the bed. Blood trickled from his nose and his jaw went numb. He tried to beg the soldiers to take him instead, but they ignored his pleas and left him behind on his hands and knees on the floor, bleeding from his face and bawling nonsense words of grief and rage.

Tom called out once before the soldiers carried him from the bedroom.

Gus climbed to his feet and staggered from the room and down the stairs. By the time he'd emerged outside, Tom was already on the truck with several other people that the soldiers had snatched from the surrounding houses. He recognised some of them. And then the truck pulled away as he stumbled from the front garden and into the road. The soldiers looked back at him, impassive and cold, apathetic. He saw Tom amongst the huddle of terrified abducted people. He thought he saw Tom's mouth form a recognisable shape.

Dad.

Gus ran after the truck until its lights faded into the darkness down the road. Then it was gone, off into the starless night.

The streetlamps flickered above him.

He fell to his knees, blood trickling into his mouth, and said his son's name until his voice faded to a pathetic whimper and all about him was silent.

CHAPTER ONE

Gus woke from a dream about his sick boy. He pressed his hands to his eyes and recalled Tom's face lost amidst the wrenching limbs of masked soldiers. Tom had called out, beseeching his father, begging for help, as the soldiers dragged him into the dark.

The dream had been one of many recurring dreams and nightmares in the last few weeks. Most mornings he'd wake with drying tears on his face and a grating sense of dread and hopelessness in his chest. Mornings were the worst.

Gus sat up on the camp bed and pulled the blankets aside. He lowered his head to cough wetly into his hand, trying to clear the croaking dampness in his chest. He'd heard of several cases of bronchitis and pneumonia in the refugee camp, and the rumours of people dying in their beds were hard to ignore.

He slumped on the edge of the bed and made sure not to look around too much. Some people were still lying in bed, asleep or staring into space, morose and depressed. Traumatised people packed into accommodation tents and given a ration allowance plus all the anti-depressants they needed. The inside of the tent, from its high ceiling to the flattened earthen floor, held the pungent smell of stale sweat, body odour and intestinal gas.

He'd found it was better to keep to himself and avoid interaction with the others. And it had worked for him so far. He had no wish to make friends; all of his had died in the Quarantine Zone.

Gus dressed quickly and shrugged on his coat. Each morning that he found his boots still by the bed he was surprised. He took a swig of water from the bottle kept next to his pillow then reached into one pocket of his coat and took out the blister pack of painkillers, popped two onto his palm and swallowed them with another swig. Then he closed his eyes and sighed, and didn't open them until the swaying inside his skull abated. He grabbed his holdall from next to the bed. It never left his sight because the camps were a good hunting ground for thieves. The holdall contained important things.

He made his bed and checked he'd left nothing behind. He took the walkway down the middle of the long tent and stepped outside. Grey daylight after the tepid dawn. The sky was various shades of ashen and concrete. He grimaced at the harsh voices, coughing fits, and the wailing of infants from the nearby tents. His shoulders slumped at the prospect of another day.

People milled about, fetching their meagre breakfasts or journeying to the rows of chemical toilets placed near the boundaries of the camp. He felt relieved that he didn't have to shit this morning.

He lit a cigarette from the dwindling amount in the pack and smoked it while he watched an elderly couple struggle out of their tent and make their way in the direction of the breakfast line, where stodgy porridge never left the menu and the most appetising item was cold baked beans. The old couple were crooked and thin, tired-looking and frail. He gave them a few months, at most, if they couldn't get a boarding placement up north.

He spat by his feet then stepped into the dazed ranks of the unwashed.

*

On a small area of ground between several tents, a group of people had gathered, on their knees and praying while a man in a hooded waterproof jacket stood before them, raised his arms and spoke words from a tattered Bible.

Gus watched them with something like pity. But he realised that could easily have been him, worshipping in the dirt, beseeching an unseen god. Those people were only looking for hope and comfort. Who was he to deny them? Many had taken to religion since the black rocks fell and the blight prospered in their wake. With each week a new cult was formed, but most of them ended in disputes and casual violence. Religion was good business for the conmen and the power-hungry, the sociopathic and the vain. There were always new members for the flock.

Gus had heard about a doomsday cult in Derbyshire that'd kidnapped several young children. The army had raided their commune and found everybody dead inside. Over one hundred people, still clutching the empty plastic cups they'd drunk poison-laced fruit juice from. The abducted children had been sacrificed and burned in a pile behind one of the buildings.

He passed the Red Cross tent, where kind women handed out medicine and leaflets to the maligned and sickly. A few soldiers strolled past him, cradling their rifles across their chests as they surveyed the walkways of the camp. They didn't give Gus a second look, as he pushed his hands into his pockets and stumbled across the damp ground. Morrissey's *Every Day Is Like Sunday* drifted between the tents and along the thoroughfares. A generator chugged and belched. Smoke rose from a campfire, around which men in long coats warmed their hands and complained to each other. Tired faces peered from the openings in tents, squinting at the morning. Prayer meetings and makeshift congregations. Children gathered in patches of muddy ground and played with toys. They glanced at Gus as he passed. Some of the boys had plastic toy guns and played at being soldiers. One of them pretended to be dead.

A man was crying in the shadows inside a tattered tent.

The camp was one of many for the refugees from southern England; a haven for those who'd escaped the blight. Gus was a four month veteran of this place, waiting to be assigned a boarding allocation further north. Some people had spent even longer in the camps. Some people had died in the camps.

Gus left through the front gates, nodding at the soldiers stationed outside. There was an army truck parked on the bare ground. A disembodied laugh burst through the air.

The grey sky was turning darker. He thought he could smell rain. He emerged onto the road and walked in the direction of the town. It was no more than three miles away, but the prospect of walking in the rain dulled whatever brief contentment the painkillers provided.

He walked on, leaving the camp behind, but its stench of chemical toilets, sewer effluent and smoke followed him even as it passed out of sight beyond the fields.

He kept to the side of the road and held his thumb out, hoping for a lift as he pulled up his hood with his other hand. Slowly, the rain began falling. Thick droplets, as cold as the wind sweeping out of the hills to the east, pattered on the cracked tarmac.

Tom had liked to walk in the rain, back before the blight arrived in the south. It all seemed like another life, a fading memory, but Gus kept the thought with him and cherished it as he made his way along the road.

CHAPTER TWO

A passing truck driver offered Gus a lift. The man was transporting medical supplies to a hospital a little further south, and in the time before he dropped Gus at the town, he regaled him with stories of his military adventures in the Middle East. Gus kept glancing at the red skull and crossbones tattoo on his left forearm. The man told Gus about the people he'd killed. Gus kept his responses to a minimum and was glad when they parted company.

The truck roared away down the road and left him standing in exhaust fumes. Gus spat and wiped his mouth. He looked around, grimacing at the drizzle.

The town was called Mareby, and Gus wondered if it had always been such a place of dullness and silent apathy. The streets seemed to be fading in the rain. Squat buildings and roads seemed too narrow for traffic to travel in both directions. There was a smell of burnt plastic mixed with blocked gutters.

The people on the streets moved in shuffling steps. A woman in a leather jacket stood outside a newsagent's and rolled a cigarette between yellowed fingers. A school bus devoid of children struggled down a road lined with parked cars. The driver raised one hand at Gus, as if they knew each other, but Gus didn't respond, and just turned away. A police car passed at no more than a crawl, the officers inside watching for trouble. One of them was chewing something and smiling to himself.

Gus walked the streets, avoiding eye contact with other people, until he arrived at the working men's club. It was a Victorian building of grey stone and darkened windows, cracked guttering and flaking paintwork. He cleared his throat to get the attention of the old man sweeping the front steps, and spoke the name of the woman on the piece of crumpled paper he'd pulled from his pocket.

The old man scowled and told him to go around the back of the club.

Gus thanked him, but the old man had already turned away.

*

Gus took the alleyway at the side of the building and emerged into a wide yard cluttered with empty beer barrels, patio furniture and rusting bicycles. There was a Ford Fiesta with flat tyres. The sound of something dripping put him on edge. He recognised the smell of cigarette ash and engine oil. A mangy dog watched him from the doorway of a kennel. The name on the kennel read **CHESTER**.

Gus knocked three times on the door, and when no one answered he pressed the buzzer and waited. He was glancing back at the dog when the door opened, and he faced the dreadlocked man glaring at him from the doorway.

"Yeah?" the man said, bunching his shoulders and frowning.

"Uh, I'm here to see Maggie."

"Maggie?"

"Yeah."

"You got an appointment?"

"Yeah, I think so."

"You think so?"

"Yeah."

"What's your name?"

"Gus Abernathy…"

The man sniffed, as if to smell Gus's scent. "Wait here."

"Okay."

The man closed the door. Gus waited. He looked over his shoulder to ensure Chester was still in his kennel. A pair of gleaming canine eyes considered him, maybe as lunch or a chew toy.

The door opened again and the dreadlocked man reappeared. "Come in. Maggie's waiting for you."

*

Gus followed the man up a stairway carpeted with some lurid floral design from the 1970s. He held onto the banister like he was afraid of falling. From other rooms of the building, jumbled voices rose and fell, muffled by the walls and ceilings.

They reached the landing without conversation.

The dreadlocked man pointed down the corridor towards a yellow door. "There."

Gus nodded. "Thanks."

The man winked at Gus. "Be careful. She's hungry." He went back down the stairs and out into the back yard. Gus heard him calling to the dog.

The floor stretched away from him. The carpet was thin enough to be no more than a layer of fuzz over the floorboards, which creaked as he walked down the corridor. He stopped outside the yellow door. It was ajar and retained the smell of fresh paint. Weak light edged through the narrow gap between the door and the jamb.

He knocked slowly, and quietly, because he thought it was wise to not appear too brash.

A man's voice answered: "Open the door, fella."

Gus did as he was told and entered the room.

CHAPTER THREE

Gus sat on the chair and looked at the old woman bundled up in a tartan blanket on the other side of the table. He had been expecting Maggie to be younger and more imposing, but here was this frail effigy of a woman with crooked limbs and hardly any meat on her bones. He placed his hands on the scuffed surface and offered a polite smile. It was the sort of table used for a séance, he thought to himself.

Maggie frowned at him over her blanket. Her grey hair was tied in a messy bun that jutted from the top of her head. Her face was drawn and mean. The teeth in her shrivelled mouth worried Gus; he suppressed a shiver as he pictured them seizing upon his throat to rip and tear.

Four men flanked the decrepit matriarch, two either side. They didn't take their eyes from Gus. The two men to the woman's left were tall and thin; the two to her right were squat and bulky. A young girl in blonde pigtails stood slightly behind Maggie and held a cigarette between the old woman's jerky-meat lips. The girl eyed Gus, her mouth curled in a scowl.

The men wore black suits, while the girl was clad in a black dress, as though they were waiting for the old woman to die so they could attend the funeral and get it over with.

Maggie sucked on the cigarette, and when the girl removed it from her creased opening of a mouth, she exhaled a cloud of blue-grey smoke that rose to the ceiling and formed a haze around the bare lightbulb.

Gus swallowed, tried to slow the kicking of his heart.

Maggie leaned forward in her blanket until her chin was above the table. "You were lucky to get an appointment." Her words were spat from smoke-damaged vocal cords. Gus resisted the urge to recoil from her leathery face.

"I know," he said. "Thank you for seeing me."

"It's short notice too."

"I really appreciate it."

Maggie nodded, sitting back in her chair. She took another drag from the girl's hand. "You're from the local camp, I assume. You look like you live in the camp. One of the refugees from down south, I bet. How do you like Derbyshire?"

"The weather's a bit shit."

Maggie snorted. "That's true. Where did you live before the outbreak?"

"Salisbury."

"That'll be quite a trek into the Quarantine Zone."

Gus glanced at the men either side of Maggie then back at her. "I would have hired a boat to take me to the west coast, so I could travel across, but there are too many Navy ships patrolling the water around the mainland. I don't mind walking."

"Fair enough." Maggie pulled the blanket tighter around her thin shoulders. "But it's not the walking you have to worry about."

"With all respect, that's not your concern."

Maggie nodded as her feeble mouth pulled at the cigarette. The girl holding it was silent, watching the smoke drift in the air. "Okay. But you should know that you won't be the first grieving father or husband to go into the Quarantine Zone. You should also know that, as far as I'm aware, no one has returned from there."

"Can we just get down to business?"

With one leathery hand, Maggie waved the girl away. The girl left the room, smoking the crumpled nub of the cigarette as she went.

"This won't be cheap," said Maggie.

"I have some savings," Gus replied.

"Good. You'll need them."

"How much will this cost?"

Maggie placed her hands upon the table and laid them flat so Gus could see her scarred knuckles, and the purple-blue veins knotted under the skin. "Five grand."

The fee would wipe out most of his savings. Not that his savings mattered anymore.

"Deal," he said.

Maggie offered a self-satisfied smile. "I like it when business is done quickly."

"Especially when you're the one getting a load of money."

Maggie snorted. "Are you immune?"

"Immune?"

"To the blight..."

"Yeah, I'm immune."

"There aren't many of your kind around."

"That's because most of my kind were taken by the government when they tried to make a vaccine."

"I heard that didn't go too well," Maggie said.

"That's what I heard, too."

"You're not a carrier?"

He shook his head. "I've been tested."

"Good for you."

"So, when do you want the money?"

Maggie tapped one finger on the table and sucked on her teeth. "Before the end of the week. One of my boys will give you the account number for the transfer."

"How do I know you'll keep your end of the deal?"

"You don't," Maggie said. "But what other choice do you have? You won't get into the Quarantine Zone by your own means. The wall stretches across the country. You won't get past the army patrols and the watchtowers. You need our help."

Any attempt to sneak over the wall would end with a sniper's bullet. "Okay. What happens now?"

"You wait for us to contact you. One of the boys will be in touch once the money's been transferred." She paused as she placed her hands together. "You can go now, Mr Abernathy."

Gus stood and stepped back from the table. "Thank you."

The old woman grinned. "Good luck. I hope you find whatever you're searching for."

CHAPTER FOUR

He transferred the money the next day, and two days later when he'd convinced himself he'd been fleeced for his savings, he received a text on the cheap mobile he'd purchased from a market stall. He sat on the edge of his bed and read the message:

Transfr compltd. Mt in Mareby town cntre by council offices, 7 pm tomorow. Dont b L8.

Gus put the phone away. He went outside and lit a cigarette, but was suddenly too nervous to smoke it, so he just stood by the entrance and looked up at the darkening sky, and did so until the stars appeared in their countless numbers.

*

The next night, which was bitterly cold, two men he recognised from his meeting with Maggie picked him up from Mareby town centre in a white Ford Transit van. One man was tall and thin, the other short and fat. They hurried Gus into the back of the van and told him to sit on the floor. The fat man took Gus's rucksack, which included a torch and other useful things, then placed a blindfold over his eyes.

"It's so you don't memorise the route," the fat man said, sniffling. His breath was rank in Gus's face.

Gus nodded, said nothing.

"Don't worry – I won't steal anything from your rucksack or your pockets. Now, just sit back and relax. We could have a game of I-Spy, but I don't think you'd be much good at it. Ha-ha."

"Shut the fuck up, Lionel," the thin man said from the driver's seat. "And sit down. I don't want your fat arse rolling about in the back of the van."

Lionel laughed and slapped Gus on the shoulder. He leaned in, close to Gus. "Ignore ol' Walter up there; he's in a bad mood because his missus just left him for a road sweeper."

"Shut the fuck up, arsehole," Walter said.

Lionel laughed again.

Gus gritted his teeth and hoped the journey wouldn't take too long.

*

They drove for a few hours, in silence, until they reached their destination. When Gus was taken from the van and his blindfold was removed, he found himself in a narrow country lane flanked by tall trees. The van was parked under the bough of a large oak. The sky was clear, and moonlight broke past the skeletal branches to paint the ground in silvery patches. A fox barked from beyond the black thickets. Gus grabbed his rucksack.

The three men switched on their torches. Walter pointed his torch towards the end of the lane. "This way."

"Where are we going?" Gus said.

Lionel slapped him on the shoulder. The man's face was severe in the torchlight.

"You'll find out, mate. Don't worry – we've done this before."

Gus looked at Lionel and said nothing. His teeth chattered.

Lionel gestured forward with his hand. "After you, mate."

Gus followed Walter down the lane. Lionel kept pace behind him, whistling a jaunty tune. A knot of dread formed in Gus's stomach. He lifted up the front of his woollen hat and wiped cold sweat from his brow. Then he quickened his pace to keep up with Walter.

*

They walked for over a mile until the ground began to fall away and they descended a wooded escarpment where the trees closed in and gave the men little room to move. They halted and looked through the sparse canopy as a helicopter passed high above, its rotor blades shuddering, tail-light blinking red in the night.

Eventually the ground levelled out again and they walked on for another half a mile before Walter pointed his torch ahead and halted. They were in some sort of clearing amongst the trees.

"This is the spot," Walter said. "We're less than three miles from the edge of the Quarantine Zone." He directed his torchlight near his feet and crouched. With one gloved hand he began brushing away dead leaves and dirt until he uncovered a round metal hatch in the ground. With a crowbar Walter prised the hatch lid from its seal and pulled it open. A rush of stinking air rose from the opening. Walter spat then peered into the hole with his torch.

Lionel stepped beside Gus and placed one hand on his shoulder. "I hope you're not claustrophobic, mate."

*

Lionel closed the hatch, and they descended the ladder into a wide tunnel. The rungs of the ladder had been greasy with some sort of fluid, and Gus could still feel it on his hands no matter how much he wiped them on his coat.

Their torches were feeble against the swarming dark. They stepped over greyish puddles on the concrete floor. There was a smell like fungal rot mixed with stagnant water. Something was dripping. The black pipes running along the tunnel walls creaked and moaned, glistening with damp and filth-slime.

Walter glanced both ways of the tunnel then gestured for Gus and Lionel to follow him. In single file they moved down the tunnel. Gus shivered, his heartbeat throbbing in his ears, the straps of his rucksack already biting into his shoulders. The nervous tension in his stomach made him nauseous, so he tried to focus his attention on following Walter's footsteps down the tunnel.

Lionel began whistling a tune again. It sounded vaguely familiar, like an old pop song. Gus wished he would stop, but didn't say anything. He pictured the trees in the ground above them, and nocturnal animals prowling through copses and thickets. He imagined soldiers patrolling the edge of the quarantine zone.

Eventually the tunnel ended at a stone wall, in which a small, horizontal hatch gleamed dully with moisture. It was barely large enough for one person.

Walter aimed his torch at the hatch then turned to Gus. Lionel stopped whistling.

"This is where we part company," Walter said.

Lionel snorted. "Yeah, this is as far as we go."

Walter frowned at the fat man. "You couldn't fit in there anyway."

"Fuck you," Lionel said, and let out a burst of laughter that echoed around them.

Gus stared at the hatch. It felt like the walls were crowding him from both sides. He exhaled deeply. His knees trembled.

"Are you okay?" Walter said.

Gus looked at him. "Yeah, I think."

Walter opened the hatch and looked inside. He appraised Gus with narrow eyes. "This tunnel will take you two miles into the Quarantine Zone. It becomes a bit of a maze, so remember to follow the yellow arrows painted on the walls. Okay?"

"Okay."

"All you have to do is crawl, my friend."

"Watch out for the rats," Lionel said. "And the spiders."

Gus nodded, swallowing, his throat dry. "Doesn't the government know about this tunnel?"

Walter spat. "They've got bigger things to worry about, I think. Riots in the cities and food shortages in the refugee camps. Influenza spreading in the north-east. The terrorist bombing in Liverpool. It's all going to shit."

"They managed to seal the other tunnels," said Lionel. "But they missed this one. Anyway, like Walter said, this little tunnel is the least of their worries."

Gus nodded again. "Okay." As the men watched, he climbed into the narrow tunnel and lay on his stomach, praying that his torch wouldn't fail him. He managed to look back over his shoulder at the men.

"Good luck," said Walter. "We won't meet again."

Lionel raised one hand and waved.

The closing of the hatch door echoed down the tunnel, and such a sense of loneliness overcame Gus that he didn't move for a long while and just lay there staring at the darkness ahead.

CHAPTER FIVE

He followed the first yellow arrow, crawling while he gasped for breath in the coffin-like confines of the tunnel. Sweat dampened his clothes. His shoulders and limbs scraped at the walls as he pulled himself along like a mole through lightless depths, groping with his hands, huffing and grunting on his hands and knees. The beam of his torch reached only several yards before it was consumed by the dark. Panic and hysteria scratched at the back of his mind, waiting to emerge, bristling with glee within the red insides of his skull.

And it was a tortuous journey. He had to stop every few minutes and wait for his breathing to slow. His heart capered with palpitations, and acidic bile frothed in his stomach. He thought he might die in these nameless tunnels, and the next person to try returning to the Quarantine Zone would find his mummified remains blocking the way.

He looked for the next yellow arrow, starkly aware of all those tonnes of dirt and stone pressing down on the tunnel. The weight of ages. Sweat trickled into his eyes. He breathed in a mouthful of dust and stifled a cry in his throat as he imagined miles of tunnel awaiting him.

It would be so easy to just lie down and give up.

*

At one point he was sure he'd lost his way. He scraped along the tunnel, grazing his elbows and knees while struggling forward. His bowels were full of shivery heat. He imagined some terrible figure of rag and bone haunting the dark tunnels. Maybe he would die and some trace of his consciousness would be trapped in this lightless maze for all time, tortured and lost, mad and hopeless, and he'd become that thing of rag and bones.

But then he happened upon a yellow arrow showing him the way, and he let out a burst of hysterical laughter that scared him more than the image of a ghoul coming up

44

behind him to grab at his legs. And after what seemed like several hours of sliding along the tunnel he emerged into a cramped underground room, where metal latticework and huddled water pipes stretched across the ceiling. He climbed down to the concrete floor, exhausted and breathing hard, and crouched with his hands at his face. His elbows and knees were sore. Aches shuddered down his spine and down the back of his legs. He stood and stretched, relieved to be out of the tunnel.

He looked around. A metal ladder leading up to ground level was the only way out. He climbed the ladder, gripping the rungs with trembling hands, careful not to let his feet slip. When he reached the top of the ladder, he opened the metal hatch.

He expected daylight, but there was only more darkness.

CHAPTER SIX

Gus climbed out of the hatch and swung his torch around, hands trembling, as he turned slowly in a circle. It was a basement of some kind, as lightless as the tunnels he'd escaped, and the cracked concrete floor was littered with hollow insect carapaces.

Cobwebs thick with dust, the tombs of their arachnid architects. The stink of animal urine was acrid in his nostrils.

On one of the dank walls, someone had scrawled WELCOME HOME in white spray paint. A smiley face painted next to the words. The eyes had run, and seemed to Gus like tendrils squirming out of its face.

He climbed a tall flight of metal steps to a higher level and took out the black-handled lock knife he'd bought from a Polish man out of a dosshouse. He moved through pitch black corridors under sagging ceilings, glancing about the darkness, until he emerged into the cavernous surroundings of a factory floor abandoned long before the evacuation.

Ruined and rusted machinery, like the corpses of steampunk war engines. Giant cogs and skeletal structures. Great machines and long production lines not used in decades. Everything derelict, corroding and covered in dust, all blackened and crumbling. Moonlight-tinged darkness revealed the shattered windows. The wind whispered through fractures in the walls, skittering through the dust, dirt and trash that carpeted the floor. Graffiti symbols and nihilistic messages adorned scarred brickwork.

He glimpsed the night sky through holes in the roof, fragments of the constellations. There was utter silence. He took a moment and just stood there, holding the knife. He felt like a ghost in this dead place.

At the back of his mind, a niggling thought suggested that he'd emerged short of the quarantine zone and been tricked by Maggie and her people. It remained there like an itch he could only scratch at with numb and useless fingers, so he stepped between the hulking shapes of dead machines and made his way outside through a fire exit door left ajar by the last soul to depart this place.

He found himself in a wide yard, standing in empty parking bays. Litter drifted along the ground, pushed by the breeze. Beyond the yard was a gravel car park revealed by the wan moonlight. Empty and desolate. Past the car park was a high wall, and further along was a set of broad gates leading out of the property. They appeared to be hanging open.

He considered setting off straight away, but he was reluctant to travel at night. He checked his wristwatch: nearly four in the morning. A few hours before dawn. He decided he would wait until first light before leaving, as he was exhausted and aching, and some rest would prepare him for the walk ahead.

*

Back inside the abandoned factory he climbed an old metal stairway to an office overlooking the ground floor. A small room with big windows, where a supervisor or shift manager would have surveyed the factory floor. In the carpet were four small square imprints left by the legs of a desk now long gone. He swept the torchlight about the walls. Bare shelves. A framed certificate awarded to *Les Powley, Supervisor of the Year, 1985*. The glass over the certificate was cloudy with blemishes, and the frame was dust-furred and stained.

He thought he could smell cigarette smoke; or at least the ghost of it from long ago.

In one corner of the office he found a pile of invoices and order forms covered in dust. Scattered paperclips and scraps of cardboard. One of the invoices was dated *October 29th, 1987*. Gus snorted, shrugged, then bunched the piece of paper into a ball and dropped it by his feet. That day had been his seventh birthday.

He closed the door and looked out across the dark factory floor. He kept his knife ready, in case he heard footsteps coming up the metal stairs.

*

Gus left the factory at first light, moving south as he checked his pocket compass. Dawn arrived in tones of dismal grey. A bank of black cloud loomed to the west. He ate a cereal bar as he walked, then pulled his cotton mask up to cover his nose and mouth. His food supplies were meagre and wouldn't last long. There were four one-litre bottles of water in his rucksack, which would have to last him.

Last until when...? When you die out here, searching for your dead son?

He ignored the voice and carried on. The road from the factory led him through an industrial estate and eventually through the outskirts of a village. All was silent, except for the dull slap of his boots on the tarmac. A few cars lined the sides of the road, long-abandoned and sagging on deflating tyres under the shadows of overhanging birch trees. Patches of black blight stained the land. He passed a house that had been hollowed out by fire, blackened and crumbling. The chimney lay in pieces on the charred front lawn.

The wind travelled down the roads and between buildings. No sign of life. Not even birds or rats. He felt terribly alone.

But at least there were no bodies, and he glimpsed only scattered bones in the weeds before he turned away and focused on the road ahead.

CHAPTER SEVEN

Gus found a road sign and checked his map. The village was called Blunsdon, and wasn't far north of Swindon, which meant he was roughly three miles inside the Quarantine Zone. Salisbury, where he and Tom lived before the outbreak, was almost forty miles away.

He wondered if anyone was still alive in the Zone, even animals or birds. Along the safe side of the border to the blighted south, the army had culled large numbers of birds to reduce the chances of them spreading the blight to the Midlands and further north. Thousands had been killed. And so far there were no reported cases of the blight outside the Zone. The cull seemed to have worked.

Gus had been walking for several hours. His pace was slowing to a shuffle and his stomach craved food. His muscles needed sustenance. He stopped west of Swindon and rested on a bench in a small park where the local flora was festooned with the blight's black tendrils and stains. After sipping some water and wolfing down a chocolate bar, he looked across the expanse of the park towards a line of malformed trees and the terraced houses beyond. The roads were deserted. Cars were parked neatly by pavements and kerbs. There were no signs of violence or destruction here. It was like everybody had just vanished. But he knew that if he went inside any of the houses he'd likely find the dead victims of the blight.

He rose from the bench and readjusted the cotton mask over his nose and mouth. Pulled down his woollen hat so that it covered the tops of his ears. Then he left the park and carried on down the road.

*

Soon afterwards he found the first black flowers. He stopped and crouched by a nest of them growing from the damp ground at the roadside. From a distance they'd looked like orchids covered in soot – and they could have easily passed for them without closer scrutiny – but once Gus was within ten yards of them, there was no question of their provenance.

"Blight flowers," he muttered. "Christ."

He'd heard about them, in the time before the evacuation and the subsequent quarantine, but never seen them up close until now, only in photos on the internet and in newspapers. He blew air from his mouth and it rippled against the fabric of his mask. He grabbed a stick and gently poked at the flowers, tensing his shoulders as if he was worried a maw would form and open then snap shut like a carnivorous plant. But nothing happened, and he withdrew the stick then poked the flower again, just to make sure. Nothing. He noticed that the ground around him was furred with black mould. Wispy strands stirring in the breeze. It stank of sour milk.

For a moment he thought he could hear the flowers whispering to him, but he dismissed it as his imagination and stood and backed away until he was almost on the other side of the road. Then he moved on.

He didn't look back.

*

It began to rain in a sudden downpour that chased Gus to the shelter of a stalled car. He sat behind the steering wheel, relieved that there were no corpses to share this moment, and placed his rucksack on the passenger seat. A set of keys dangled from the ignition. He tried the engine, but it was dead. But he had already known this. None of the vehicles would start again. Something inside the Quarantine Zone was emitting an electromagnetic pulse. Not even planes, helicopters or drones could overfly the Zone; the ones that tried fell from the sky. There had been many deaths before the authorities figured it out. The experts suggested that it had something to do with the black rocks from the sky.

The no-fly zone stretched from just north of Bristol on the west coast, to Clacton-Upon-Sea in the east. Even planes flying close to the Zone experienced engine trouble. There was even a rumour that orbiting satellites couldn't view the south of England.

A few weeks ago, the leader of the Liberal Democrats had suggested using hot air balloons to fly over and observe the Quarantine Zone, but he'd been roundly mocked in the media and the government. The newly-created Parliament in Manchester had dismissed his suggestion and moved on to the more pressing matter of the street battles between extremist Muslims and English nationalist groups in Leeds.

After a few minutes, the rain stopped, and Gus climbed outside and stood in the road as he shouldered his rucksack. He left the car behind and moved on, watching the sky and noting the fading of the light.

CHAPTER EIGHT

Gus had walked over ten miles on that first day in the Quarantine Zone. He was past exhaustion by the time he stopped at a house just outside a small village south of a road crammed with traffic wrecks and dead vehicles. He could taste metal at the back of his mouth. Darkness was bleeding in at the edges of the world. He had seen more black flowers as he walked, and had kept his distance from them. He'd been sure that the flowers had twitched and whispered at his presence, but he didn't hang around to confirm it.

He broke into the house and stood in the hallway, the torch and the lock knife in either hand. An old bicycle propped against the wall at the foot of the stairs. Piles of newspapers on the floor. He searched the downstairs rooms, and was relieved to find no bodies. An old couple had lived here, according to the photos on the walls, the tops of bureaus and desks. When he stepped out into the back garden he discovered an old, collapsing funeral pyre long burnt-out and blackened. He looked down at the charred human bones amongst the carbonised sticks and scorched grass. A skull nestled in the ashes, eye sockets gaping, crisped by the fire.

He returned inside the house. Before he closed the back door he looked back at the cold pyre and thought he could smell the smoke ghosts of its long ago burning.

*

Upstairs he found two bedrooms and a bathroom where the walls were the worst shade of brown he'd ever seen. He hesitated before he drew back the shower curtains, but there was nobody inside. He found some prescription painkillers in the mirrored cupboard above the sink and pocketed them after he checked the labels for their use-by-dates.

He sat at the table in the dining room and ate his dinner. Cold beans spooned from a tin, with tinned peaches for dessert. He drank water until his stomach was swollen and he sat back in his chair in a contented daze.

He smoked a cigarette and watched the darkness fill the windows.

*

Gus spent the night in the smaller bedroom, uneasy and squirming under the dusty sheets. He had left the doors unlocked, and only remembered this when he woke just after two in the morning from a dream in which Tom had walked the road with him.

He was too tired to move, so he went back to sleep. Tom was absent from the dreams that followed.

*

The morning was mostly rain and sleet, falling against the windows and upon the roof. He raised the hood of his coat and the cotton mask over his mouth and nose. Hung his rucksack over one shoulder. Then he stood in the front doorway, looking out at the grim day. The prospect of walking the roads in the downpour instilled a sense of creeping despair in his gut.

As the rain lessened and slowed, he stepped outside, closed the door and started across the garden and towards the road. But when he was halfway down the path he stopped and turned, then walked back to the house.

He had an idea.

CHAPTER NINE

It took a while to find a hand pump so he could inflate the bicycle's tyres. He oiled the chain and checked the brakes, then wheeled it outside onto the road. It looked like one of the old road bicycles he'd ridden when he was a boy. The tyres were narrow and had minimal tread; he would have to be careful on the wet roads. The handlebars curved forward and down, and the frame weighed little in his hands, like it was made of cardboard.

He hesitated before he swung one leg over the bicycle and perched upon the seat. He gripped the handlebars and hunched slightly forward, then pushed with his foot and started down the road.

*

He took the bicycle onto the A346 road, which would take him south to Salisbury. He hoped to reach his old house before dusk. Stalled vehicles littered the road, and he rode slowly around them. Cars lined the roadside for hundreds of yards. Roof-racks laden with bags and suitcases, with no sign of their owners or anybody else. This was the land of the abandoned and the dead.

A mangy fox bolted across the road ahead without glancing at Gus. He watched it slink into a field of tall grass and dense thickets.

Cold air gnawed at his face. His eyes watered as he clicked through the gears and made his way along the silent road. He'd been riding for twenty minutes under a grey sky of incessant rain when he braked gently and guided the bicycle to the side of the road. His attention was caught by the copse of twisted, blight-infected oaks in the middle of the adjacent field.

"What do we have here?"

Several dozen crows had alighted on the trees' skeletal branches, all watching Gus. They were unmoving, like forms of shadow in the rain. Maybe they were just surprised to see a human being in the area. Perhaps they had gotten used to the absence of people.

Maybe it was something else.

He felt a low ringing in his ears, as though he was hearing it through a longwave radio. He shook his head and rubbed his eyes with the heels of his hands, and when he looked back at the crows, they were still watching him.

Their beady, onyx-like eyes followed him as he moved on.

*

The ringing in his ears eventually faded. A few miles on, Gus had to dismount when he arrived at a section of road blocked by dead traffic. He wheeled the bicycle between sagging vehicles and made sure not to look at the indistinct forms huddled and sprawled beyond windows blurred with rainwater.

The trees at the roadsides were black and crooked from the blight, and blotchy with pale yellow lichen. The grass beneath their gnarled boughs was discoloured and bristling with disease. The blight was still spreading, consuming the land, and he wondered if it would eventually spread from the Quarantine Zone. He imagined the entire planet infected.

After passing through the ranks of dead cars, buses and trucks, he climbed back onto the bike and started working the pedals. The road opened ahead, and he glanced around and kept one eye on the tarmac, careful to avoid the potholes and wide cracks before him.

When he looked to his left, towards the western sky, he saw a flock of crows rise from beyond the trees. And he pedalled faster because he was sure they were the same crows he'd encountered back down the road and they were watching him again.

*

He made his way through more towns and villages, all of them deserted and silent save for scurrying rats and the occasional pigeon scavenging through dead leaves and trash. He watched for the crows, but they had withdrawn from sight, and he dismissed his concerns as mere paranoia.

The rain came and went, but never left for too long, and by the time he reached the outskirts of Salisbury and the dark shape of the cathedral spire announced itself from beyond the houses, he was soaked to the skin. The last time he'd seen his hometown he'd watched it recede behind him from the back seat of a National Express coach taking civilians northwards.

Unsurprisingly no one was there to greet him. The main road into Salisbury was empty of vehicles down to the next roundabout, but he guessed that would change the further he went into the city.

There was the stench of pungent rot on the breeze, even though there were no corpses in sight. But Gus knew that the silent rooms of houses held the corpses of the dead, the former inhabitants of the city.

CHAPTER TEN

Gus walked into Salisbury, pushing the bicycle alongside him. He glanced around, watching the windows of buildings that he passed. The wind slipped down deserted streets, scattering plastic bags and scraps of paper, wailing in a high-pitched tone through alleys and passageways.

Crows watched him from rooftops and the tops of high walls. He tried to ignore them.

The city spoke to him with its deafening silence. It was like a weight on his shoulders. He walked roads he recognised from before the evacuation, and shops he once frequented. The newsagent's where he used to buy his cigarettes and gin. The houses of friends he used to know. Places he used to know. He pictured his boy running through the streets, laughing and whooping, and wiped his damp eyes.

He passed his old workplace; the factory was falling into disrepair. Moss-like patches of the blight were pushing through the surface of the car park. And when he passed Tom's school and the sweeping abandonment of the silent playgrounds, he suppressed a heaving sob by placing his knuckles into his mouth. He looked to the windows of the long, wide building, but no faces peered out from the classrooms.

All the while, the cathedral spire loomed above the rooftops, reaching for the sky, the last monument of a dead city.

*

When he arrived at his old street, his heart quickened and he struggled to drag his legs forward. There were tears in his eyes as he walked. Flashbulb images of his son burst inside his mind. The phantom call of Tom's voice on the wind.

The neighbours' houses were dark and silent. Nothing moved. Weeds were beginning to flourish within cracks in the road and pavements. He wondered if people would ever return to the city and the blighted south. Perhaps it would be left to ruin.

The trees at one side of the road were infected with the blight. Parts of them looked to be rotting. Their branches were twisted and sharp. It had spread to some of the gardens, where the lawns were speckled black and diseased. Even a few of the window frames at the front of houses were tainted with blemishes of black mould.

He stood at the garden gate of his house, looking up the pathway at the front door. The overgrown lawn and the house beyond appeared untouched by the blight, but it was little consolation, and the air seemed thick with its particles. He said Tom's name and clenched one hand into a fist and exhaled deeply. No point in wiping his eyes. He waited for Tom to appear at a window, but despite waiting for a while, he was left disappointed. Did he really think Tom was still alive? Had his sustained grief reduced him to blindly hoping against hope for his son to be here?

He realised that the dreams meant nothing. He slumped.

Gus opened the gate and walked up the pathway.

*

And still a small part of his mind hoped that Tom would appear to welcome him home. He stood, blinking in the slow fading of the light. He crouched and took the door key from beneath the base of the bearded gnome with the fishing rod. He turned the key over in his fingers then pushed it into the lock and opened the door. He hesitated at the threshold to his home, his real home, and breathed in the stale air meeting him from the familiar rooms. With one foot forward he was inside, onto the dark brown carpet, and he closed the door and stood there, almost expecting Tom to come running down the stairs to greet him with a rib-bruising hug.

But there was just the empty house and the faded memories. The walls he knew but had not known for months. Light switches and coat hooks, lightbulbs and skirting boards. A half-smile, bittersweet and uncertain, trembled at one corner of his mouth. He felt a little sick. A weakness in his knees.

He shivered in the cold, and let his feet take him back in time.

CHAPTER ELEVEN

He thought he could smell the particular scent of his boy, and wondered if he was slowly losing his mind, with brain cells and neurons dying in the heat of encroaching madness. Maybe it would be for the best. Maybe that was the way it was supposed to be.

He searched the downstairs rooms, trailing one hand upon the walls, moving through echoes of memories of dreams, still expecting to see Tom every time he turned a corner.

Everything covered in a thick layer of dust. The glass in the windows was intact. And then he climbed the stairs and stood in Tom's bedroom. He couldn't hear his heart. He looked down at Tom's bed, which he'd remade after Tom had been taken away by the soldiers.

Posters of footballers remained on the walls. Action figures in ranks on the shelves near the window. Football programmes and magazines. A pile of Marvel comics. An Argos catalogue upon a stool, opened on the toys section.

All these old things. Gus sat on the edge of the bed and put his hands to his face. He looked at the floor. The mattress made sounds as he shifted. All he wished for was to lie down on the bed and grasp what little remained of his son.

"Tom," he said, and his voice no more than a trembling whisper. "I'm sorry, Tom. My boy. My beautiful boy."

*

He found a forgotten bottle of gin in a kitchen cupboard and sank a fourth of it while slumped on the floor. After he lit a cigarette he left the house to wander the streets in the growing dark. The alcohol burned his throat, but soothed the shaking of his hands; and by the time he'd walked two streets from his house he was already stumbling along the road. The swimming thoughts in his mind were mostly incoherent.

The streets echoed with Tom's name as Gus shouted it towards the sky. The silent, dead city, darkening around him like he was inside a hole gradually being filled in with dirt. He looked to the emerging stars and felt the incomprehensible void of the universe reach out and crush the soft parts inside him. The blight had come from the endless dark, a visitor with the worst of gifts. Maybe it would return there, once it was done with this little planet.

Gus's boots scraped upon the road as he dragged his feet, swigging from the gin bottle as indistinct memories of Tom swam through his mind. He was beyond distraught, wiping his eyes with the back of his hand. The cigarette burned down to a glowing nub between his fingers, so he flicked it away and it vanished into the growing shadows.

Dusk grew colder around him.

He stopped in the road when he smelled ammonia on the air. He took a breath and coughed, then took another shot of gin to wash away the acrid taste in his throat. And when he looked down the road in the failing light, a thin shape emerged from behind a wrecked car and stood there watching him.

It was a little girl in a red polka-dot dress and trilby hat. Her skin was blackened, like she'd suffered terrible burns.

Gus thought he was hallucinating. He scoffed, shook his head, muttered under his breath.

The girl held out one hand, as if to ask him for something. Her face was creased with sadness.

A high-pitched ringing began between Gus's ears, spreading to vibrate through his skull, into his teeth, and it was all he could do to stay on his feet. He dropped the gin bottle. It smashed on the road into a dozen shards of glass. He looked down at it, regretful he had wasted good gin.

"Come closer," the girl said. Gus regarded her through eyes prickling with the pain from inside his head. She had to be in her early teens, not much older than Tom. Strands of straw-like hair slipped from underneath the brim of her trilby. The narrow slit of her mouth was bloodless and elongated. A spark of colour in her eyes, like the last dying ember in a campfire. The blackened skin flaked from parts of her face.

"Who are you?" Gus asked. "I thought everyone was dead."

"I'm just a little girl. Won't you help me? I'm hungry and cold. Please help me."

Gus stepped towards the girl, overcome with sympathy for her, until something changed in her face and he froze.

Her sorrowful expression became a wolfish grin, which curled upwards to just below her eyes. Some teeth were glimpsed, and they seemed perfectly white.

The smell of ammonia grew stronger. The incessant ringing became louder.

The girl opened her mouth very wide, and at the back of her throat, past her pristine teeth, a yellowish light bloomed. It filled her mouth as her jaws unhinged and drooped. Gus stared in horror, the pain in his head pulsing with a dozen heartbeats, drowning out his thoughts.

The holes in the girl's face were aglow with the ghost light.

Gus gripped his head and made a sound like a slowed-down groan.

The girl shrieked and reached for him with blackened hands. Her voice was in his head. Gus turned and stumbled away moments before she could grab him.

As he fled, he was sure the girl had been floating inches above the ground.

The girl called for him to come back, so they could dance together in the street, but he was already staggering down a side road to gasp and suffer in the thickening shadows.

*

He fled into the maze of streets and alleyways, the inside of his head a riot of sounds and images. He glimpsed figures at his flanks and all around him. Some peered from around the corners of buildings or from behind abandoned cars. They made awful sounds as they mocked and tormented him, words mixed with grunted cries and breathless giggling. Mammalian snorts and guffaws echoed out of the dark.

Shadows pointed at him then merged with other shadows. A face appeared behind the plate glass of a shop front, creased and trembling with silent laughter. Gus ran until the same girl stepped into sight ahead of him. He halted, breathing hard, hunched over with one hand to his chest.

No, it wasn't the same girl with blackened skin, because she was dressed in a blue polka-dot dress and a bowler hat too big for her. The hat came down to just above her eyes. Her mouth stretched into a malevolent grin.

"Why run?" she said. "Why not stay here with us? We haven't met anyone *new* for a while. *No one* visits anymore."

"What do you want?" Gus said through gritted teeth.

She rolled her eyes, as if it was the silliest question in the world. "Your life, of course. Your spark. Your heart."

And then her mouth and eyes began to glow with that diseased light. Gus gripped at his head as something inside fell apart like pudding, and he reeled away, eyes half-closed, until he backed into a wall.

The girl moved towards him, the light pulsing in her head. The inside of her skull burned like a monstrous lantern.

Gus arched his spine as bolts of sharp pain reduced his back to trembling meat, and he fell to his knees. He was crying. Scenes of slaughter filled his mind. The sound of infants wailing for their mothers. Frothy spit spilled from between his lips.

The high-pitched ringing rose in several octaves. In one of the shops across the street, a window cracked. Static buzzed in the air. The sky was full of crows swarming in immense numbers.

Gus screamed and put his hands to his face. Tasted blood in his mouth. It felt like a molar had cracked when he snapped his jaw shut.

He raised his head to look at the girl, who approached in small footsteps. She cocked her head to one side. And from behind and around her, the others emerged, with blackened skin and the diseased light inside their skulls. The girl in the red polka-dot dress and trilby grinned as she approached.

The ones who followed were strange-looking and just as eccentric in their fashion tastes. They wore odd garments, old-fashioned and eclectic, ill-fitting and outlandish, taken from boutiques and charity shops and clothes banks outside supermarkets. Shawls and stained shrouds, creased denim and polyester. One man wore a fedora, a velvet jacket and nothing else except the awful smile on his face. A teenage boy was staring through a pair of tinted goggles, and his tracksuit was open at the front to display a thin chest of pale skin and wispy hair. An obese woman limped towards him with the aid of a walking stick, huffing and grunting, her face burning with ghost light. She muttered, "Delightful delicious," and giggled with one hand shaking at her twisted mouth.

Spindly shapes and reaching hands. Long fingers decorated with gold rings. Hoarse whispers and gibbering exultations. Wrists encased in bracelets and broken watches. Snatches of laughter and crude insults. Moans of hunger. They looked like the ghastly apparitions of people lost in fires; things not quite alive, caught between worlds.

And they came for Gus, craving his heart and his life.

Somehow, despite his trembling arms, he managed to slip the lock knife from his pocket, and he held it up at the strange people.

They merely smiled and reached for him.

He cried.

Then the world flared blinding white and the roar of thunder filled the air.

All about him there was screaming.

Gus screamed, too.

*

The apparitions, the holes in their blackened faces aglow as they screeched and whined, retreated from Gus and fled into the shadows on the other side of the street. The only one to remain was the obese woman, who was on her knees and caught in some sort of seizure. She dropped the walking stick as her hands went to her face and she clawed at the skin on her flabby cheeks and raked away strips of skin. Blood was streaming from her glowing eyes and the shocked gaping of her mouth. Steam was rising from her skin. She fell onto all fours and slapped at the ground. Gus shrank away from her, whimpering, but he couldn't take his eyes from her convulsing form, and all he could do was watch as the flesh melted from her face and her eyes dissolved into soup that spilled down her cheekbones.

Then she collapsed to one side, her bulging stomach flopping from underneath the t-shirt. She didn't move again.

Across the street, the other freaks groaned and cowered. Some flailed their arms to the sky and let out mournful cries.

Movement to his right side caught his attention. Scuffling feet coming towards him. Small hands grabbed his shoulders and hauled him from the ground, and then he was on his feet, dazed and muttering, as the small, hooded, faceless figure dragged him out of the street and down a narrow passageway.

"Where are we going...?" he asked.

His saviour didn't answer.

*

Gus was taken to an underpass several streets away. He collapsed, disorientated and exhausted, to the dirty floor and slumped against a wall that smelled of stale urine.

The hooded figure stood over him, breathing slowly, its shoulders rising and falling. Gus looked up at the figure. Its face was obscured.

"Who are you?" Gus said. "Who were those fucking loonies back there?"

The figure stepped forward and pulled down its hood with grimy hands.

Gus stared, incapable of words. His vision whitened at the edges. He tried to speak, but all he managed was a pained murmur, and tears pooled in his eyes.

The boy smiled a sad smile. "I knew you'd find me, Dad."

CHAPTER TWELVE

Gus opened his mouth to say his boy's name, but an intense pain filled his chest and he convulsed and groaned, gritting his teeth. He pressed one hand over his heart, which felt like it was being pierced by hot needles.

Tom crouched beside Gus and gently pulled his hand from his chest. Then he placed his own hands over his father's heart.

"Close your eyes."

Gus looked at him, confused.

"Just do it, Dad."

Gus closed his eyes.

The pain began to fade, chased from his chest by a cooling sensation that was not unpleasant. And by the time he opened his eyes, the pain was gone and he just sat there taking deep breaths as he stared at his son.

Tom withdrew his hands and placed one on Gus's shoulder. He smiled, and the expression broke Gus's heart.

"What happened?" Gus said. Sweat covered his face and dripped from his chin. His body ached and rattled. A great tiredness pressed at his eyes. The inside of his head felt like it was full of cotton wool and rags. Tom's face blurred then defined itself into lines and soft angles. Gus wiped his eyes to clear them, but it seemed like the air was wavering with heat.

"It's okay, Dad," said Tom, keeping his voice low. He glanced at both entrances to the underpass.

Gus was shaking his head, rubbing at the bridge of his nose. Trembling with shock and the cold air, he wiped his mouth. His jaws throbbed. "Is it okay?"

"Yes, Dad; we just have to wait here and see what happens."

*

And they waited for a short while, but the people with blackened skin did not come for them. Tom helped Gus to his feet and together they crept out into the silent street.

"Where are we going?" Gus said.

"I have a place," Tom answered. "We'll be safe. They won't find us there."

CHAPTER THIRTEEN

They walked the dark streets without a word. Gus couldn't believe he was holding Tom's hand. This couldn't be happening. Part of him refused to believe, as if it was a dream, or he was close to death and hallucinating. He kept shaking his head, and his mouth was creased with a smile that felt strange and numb upon his face. He hadn't smiled in a long time. Not a real smile.

The sky was full of stars, and the light from those burning sky-fields was enough to show them the way to Tom's hideout. The city sighed in the night as wind slipped down streets and roads, between buildings and across empty spaces.

Silent houses with windows the shade of deep water. Overgrown gardens in the pale moonlight. Gus watched the shadows for movement, but they remained motionless and solemn, and no terrible figures shrouded in blackened skin and charity shop clothes emerged with intentions for his heart.

"I've missed you, son," Gus said.

Tom glanced at him then watched the street again. "I've missed you, too, Dad."

"This doesn't seem real."

"It is real, Dad, don't worry."

"I don't understand."

"You will soon, Dad. I'll tell you everything."

*

Tom said his hideout was in the back room of a sweet shop near the city centre. When they arrived they walked around to the rear of the shop to an alleyway and entered the backyard through some loose panels in the wooden fence. Tom had a key for the back door. Gus watched the boy fiddle with the lock until the door gave way. They entered the building. Tom closed the door behind him and locked it, then took a small torch from his pocket and turned it on and aimed it down a dusty corridor. Gus remembered that he'd left his rucksack and torch back where he'd been attacked. He realised that he didn't care much, because he'd found Tom and that was all that mattered.

They followed the corridor to a small room. Tom lit the lantern in the corner. Blankets and a sleeping bag were scattered on the floor, along with sweet wrappers and plastic bags full of chocolate bars and crisps. A pile of photo albums to one side of the room. A beanbag chair sagged in the middle of the floor, among the toys that Tom had taken from his bedroom. Action figures and notepads, pencils and books. The walls were covered in posters of footballers, Transformers, and dragons.

The air stank of body odour and pear drops. The room was like a nest.

Tom shut the door. Gus hugged him, held him tight. He dropped his face to the top of Tom's head and sobbed a little, breathing in the wonderful scent of his boy. Tom cried, too, and trembled against his father.

They stayed like that for a long while as the lantern glowed and froze their shadows on the walls.

*

They sat across from each other, eating crisps and chocolate, stuffing their faces until they were content. Tom grabbed two cans of supermarket-brand cola and gave one to Gus, who sank it in several gulps and sat back with a satisfied sigh. He'd downed a few painkillers before the feast, and now he was numb and comfortable. A blanket was draped around his shoulders and another underneath him. Tom had done the same.

The boy's face was shockingly pale even in the warm light of the lantern. There was a healing, pinkish scar across his forehead. His frail form clad in a dark jacket over layers of dull clothing. His eyes gleamed, watering as he finished his fizzy drink. He put the empty can on the floor and let out a small burp.

"Pardon you," said Gus.

"Pardon me," said Tom.

Gus looked around the room. "Are we safe?"

"They've never found me here."

"Who are they?"

Tom sniffled. "The Nephilim."

"Sounds mental."

"They're scattered all over the south. Little tribes of them. We were lucky back there; the ones that attacked you weren't very powerful. The stronger ones must be hunting in other places tonight."

"Hunting?"

Tom nodded. "They hunt people."

"Are they human?"

"Used to be. Not anymore."

An itch appeared at the back of Gus's throat; he craved a cigarette. "What happened to them?"

Tom bit his lower lip. "The blight did something to them. It changed them."

"The blight only kills people," said Gus.

"I'm still alive, aren't I?"

Gus didn't answer.

Tom went on: "I think they're like vampires. *Psychic* vampires, in a way. They drain the life from people...or just rip them apart, with their minds."

"You should be dead, Tom," said Gus, blinking rapidly. His heart was like thunder as he looked into the boy's face. "How did you survive? The last time I saw you, you were in the back of a truck, as the army took you away. What happened to you?"

"I can't remember very well," said Tom. "It's a bit like a dream. It's all foggy, out of focus. Bits of memories."

"What do you remember?"

"I think the truck crashed. I remember crawling away while people screamed from the wreck. I escaped. After that, I don't remember anything until recently.

"How recently?"

"The last few weeks, when I started calling to you for help."

"That was when I started having the dreams about you. It was like a signal from you. A call for help. That's why I came back."

Tom nodded. "I didn't think it would work."

"Are you like them?" said Gus. "The Nephilim?"

Tom shook his head. His eyes were glassy, reflecting the lantern's light. "I'm not sure, Dad."

"What does that mean?"

"I don't know."

"You have…capabilities, like them," said Gus. "It was you who killed that obese woman, wasn't it?"

The boy nodded, held his hands before his face. "There's something inside me, Dad, giving me these abilities. The Nephilim want it."

"What is it?" said Gus.

The boy looked away and his mouth trembled. "A god. I think it's a god."

CHAPTER FOURTEEN

Gus slept fitfully in the dark hours, squirming and shifting under the blankets. During the times he was awake he watched Tom from across the room and thought about what the boy said earlier. His relief and joy that his boy had survived was tempered by concerns for Tom's health and the fact that Tom was changed in a fundamental way. He wasn't a normal boy anymore.

Gus imagined something gestating inside Tom, its tendrils stretching and twisting around his son's spine, growing stronger until it was ready to emerge.

An embryonic god. Something born from the blight.

The thought turned his stomach and left him in a quiet moment of despair. And he mouthed Tom's name and put his hands together then bowed his head and listened to his boy's gentle breathing in sleep.

*

They ate a breakfast of crisps and chocolate, followed by a shared can of cheap lemonade.

"I'm taking you out of here," Gus said.

"Out of the Quarantine Zone?" Tom wiped his mouth. "What if I infect people? I could be a carrier for the blight."

"We don't know that would happen."

"But it could happen…"

"It may not happen."

"I've still got the blight, Dad."

"We'll figure something out."

"Like what?"

"I don't know. If it comes to it, I'll stay in the Quarantine Zone with you. I'm not letting you go again."

Tom sighed. "Okay."

"We'll be fine, Tom."

"I believe you, Dad."

"Good lad. You've got your mum's common sense."

"I miss Mum."

"I miss her, too."

"We have to go somewhere," Tom said.

"Where?"

"I've been having dreams about a place."

"What place?"

"The place where the black rocks fell. It's been calling to me. It's connected to what's inside me."

"The god?"

"Yeah."

"Why is it calling to you? What does it want?"

"I don't know, Dad."

*

After they packed some food and drink into a plastic bag, they left the sweet shop behind and set off into the streets underneath a clear blue sky. They returned to where the Nephilim attacked Gus, and found the obese woman still lying in the road. Gus's rucksack had been emptied and torn apart, and everything inside was smashed and ruined. His torch was in pieces. There was nothing salvageable, so they moved on.

They walked alongside each other, watching the early morning shadows slowly recede from the pale sunlight. There was little warmth. Gus pulled his coat tighter around his shoulders and rubbed his hands together. His breath steamed from his mouth.

"Are you sure you want to do this?" Gus looked at the boy.

Tom nodded, glancing around the left side of the street. He chewed on a liquorice whip. "We have to get out of Salisbury, anyway. The Nephilim here will find me eventually. It's not good to stay in one place. They'll kill you, drain you of life; I don't know what they'll do to me. Something worse, I imagine."

"Why do they want you?"

"The embryonic god," Tom said, as if it were the most normal thing to tell his father. "The shadow inside me. They adore it. They want to take it out of me. The process would kill me – I've seen it in my dreams. The blight made me into a host for the god, and it made them into the Nephilim. We're all linked by the blight."

"This can't be real," said Gus. "This is madness."

Tom looked at his father. His eyes glimmered within his severe and deathly pale face. He wiped his mouth. "I wish it wasn't real. I know the names of the Nephilim. I know who they were before the black rocks fell to earth. I know the names they call themselves now: the Pastor; the Ape; Red Sally; Mr Death; John Smith; Brown Suit; the Crawler; Sister Leech; and so many more, including the Gelding."

"The Gelding?"

"He's the most powerful, much more so than those that attacked you last night. They're nothing compared to him."

"Then let's hope we don't run into him," Gus said.

Tom halted in the road. Gus looked at him and did the same. Tom was staring down the street, his mouth damp, somewhere between squinting and frowning. Gus followed his gaze.

A woman with blackened and weeping skin had been tied to an office chair and left on the road like a nasty surprise for them. Her cocktail dress was ripped and filthy. She was sobbing with her head lowered to her chest. Her hair was a tall mound atop her head, scraggly and knotted, infused with sharp pins and clips.

"She's one of them," said Tom.

Gus took out his knife.

Tom shook his head and didn't move his eyes from the woman. "I don't think we'll need that, Dad."

*

They approached the woman and stopped several yards from where she trembled and groaned. She was restrained with barbed wire wrapped around her middle and the back of the chair, holding her tight with her arms at her sides. Her dress was sodden with blood, which dripped from the cuts and lacerations in her skin. She had learned not to squirm after the barbs had done their worst upon her stomach.

Gus recoiled from the woman's ammonia stench. Tom just stood there and stared at her. She moaned softly, and stirred, her head bobbling slightly as she became aware of them. Then she raised her face to display the wounds of her punishment.

Her eyes had been ripped from their sockets. Her mouth was lipless and raw, dripping wet. The movement of her tongue, behind the ruins of her shattered teeth, was mesmerising.

"Who did this to her?" Gus said.

Tom wiped his mouth with the back of one hand. "Her own kind. The Nephilim."

"Why?"

"Sometimes, if they can't find suitable prey, they turn against the weakest in the tribe. Have fun with them."

"All because I got away?" said Gus.

Tom glanced at him. There was no need to answer.

The woman whined lowly in her throat.

"They did this with their minds," Tom said. He moved towards her and reached out to her face and touched her cheek. The woman didn't react. Gus became aware of static in the air. He glanced towards a nearby car when its windows trembled in their frames.

When he looked back at Tom and the woman, the woman was making a cooing noise, much like that of an animal. Then her mouth tried to form words, but all that emerged were phlegmy grunts and snuffling mumbles.

"It's okay," Tom said to her. "I don't blame you for what you've become. It's not your fault. It's no one's fault."

Tom gripped the sides of her head with his hands and squeezed, and from his palms came a yellowish light that throbbed and rang like echoing metal.

Gus watched as an idiotic smile formed on the woman's face and the light from Tom's hands passed into her head. Tom stepped back, holding his hands together, rubbing his knuckles, as the woman uttered a low cry. Yellow-white smoke streamed from her eye sockets and she slumped forward and convulsed before finally she stopped moving and there was just the following silence.

The faded pages of a newspaper drifted across the street and stuck in a storm drain already obstructed by dead leaves and other trash. The front page read: *The Blight Spreads! The Queen is Dead!*

Tom turned to Gus, eyes damp and bloodshot. A tremor passed through his hands. His shoulders trembled.

"Are you okay?" said Gus. He wanted to put his arms around Tom and comfort the boy, but he hesitated, and by the time he moved towards Tom, his son was already walking away down the street.

Gus looked at the dead woman one last time then followed the boy, trailing in his wake, hurrying to catch up.

CHAPTER FIFTEEN

On the way out of Salisbury, they encountered two men in odd clothes loitering in a doorway. The men grinned, their charred faces encrusted with filth, weeping with pus and lymph. Broken teeth within slack mouths. They laughed with the cadence of hyenas until Tom turned and stared at them, and they shrank away inside the building, whining and yipping like pitiful beasts.

Tom turned back to the road and resumed walking. Gus moved alongside him, glancing back at the building to make sure the men hadn't returned. He looked at the houses and the ground. A knot of bittersweet angst formed in his stomach when he realised they were leaving their home behind, again. It made him feel nauseous and jittery.

And after they'd left the city and travelled for a little while, they stopped and looked back at the horizon. Tom stared, his eyes distant, head tilted slightly, as if he was listening to something Gus couldn't hear drifting from the gathered buildings and streets. An inaudible whisper hidden in the breeze like a coded message.

"You okay?" Gus said.

Tom nodded, said nothing.

They moved on, heading towards the south west and the impact site, where the black rocks had fallen.

*

It began to rain slow drops of cold water. The sky darkened until was little more than a ceiling of black cloud. A chill wind pushed the rain into Gus's face. The plastic bag full of food swung from his hand, its handle digging into his fingers. He wiped at his eyes, kept close to Tom, who was silent and staring at the road they walked upon.

"I left all my stuff behind," said Tom. He was talking to himself. "My action figures, books, comics…"

Gus put his hand on the boy's shoulder. "We can go back to get them, eventually."

Tom didn't look convinced when he turned to Gus. "That depends if we're allowed to go back."

"What do you mean by that?" Gus withdrew his hand. The rain pattered on the road.

"I don't know what will happen when we reach the impact site. I don't know what's there."

"But something's there…"

"Yes, something is there."

"Something bad?"

"Probably. Sorry."

"Don't be sorry."

"Fair enough, Dad."

*

They found withered bodies hanging from blight-infected trees either side of the road. Blackened branches swayed in the wind. The flayed bodies eased back and forth on their ropes like ghastly puppets.

Gus used his foot to prod a desiccated pile of skin and rags. When he noticed a faded tattoo on a flap of skin, he stepped away and spat.

"They were skinned alive and drained of life," said Tom. "They were screaming. The Nephilim did this." He didn't take his eyes from them. One of the bodies had been a child. No way to identify its gender, all raw, shrivelled and slick-red.

Birds had been at the meat. Gus thought he heard crows cawing in the distance.

"They were normal people," said Tom. "Just trying to survive. They were ambushed. It happened fast. They had a gun, but it was no good against the Nephilim, and there was no chance of escape."

"Come on," said Gus. "Let's move."

"I wish we could bury them," Tom muttered. "They shouldn't be up there, for all the freaks to see."

Gus said nothing, and gently took the boy with him as he started down the road.

At least the rain had stopped.

CHAPTER SIXTEEN

They walked through several deserted and silent villages before arriving at Shaftsbury just before dusk. They had travelled twenty miles and were beyond exhaustion. Tom was leaning against Gus, and Gus was happy to hold him upright and keep him on his feet.

The rain returned and fell in intermittent downpours that were as short-lived as they were intense. The town seemed empty of life, a forlorn place of silent echoes. It worried Gus to see more shrivelled corpses hanging from poles and streetlights.

"Are the Nephilim here?" he asked Tom as they sheltered under a tree.

The boy looked out at the houses in the street. Some of the houses and gardens were blackened with the blight. His eyes narrowed. A muscle twitched above his mouth. "I don't know. It's hard to tell."

The rain lessened to drizzle and eventually stopped. Gus wiped his face. "Let's find somewhere safe for the night."

"Nowhere around here is safe, Dad. Even without capabilities, you should know that."

Gus snorted then suppressed an indignant laugh. "Fair enough, lad. I'll let you pick our accommodation for tonight. Somewhere with room service."

Tom shook his head. "You're not funny, Dad."

*

They stood outside the supermarket, the light fading around them. The sky was growing darker as dusk neared. The large windows at the front of the building had been smashed, and shards of plate glass littered the walkway. Trolleys were scattered about, a few of them laden with damp cardboard and animal bones. The outer walls were charred in places and marked with graffiti symbols and insults. Tom read the words in a breathless whisper.

They walked the trashed aisles. Areas of the floor were burnt and blackened. Dark stains and mouldy patches. Bones were scattered across the floor. Gus didn't stop to study them. On the floor were patches of what appeared to be bird droppings. The acrid stink stung Gus's nostrils. He looked around, wrinkling his nose, wincing at the smell of rotted food and stagnant fluids. The store had been looted bare, and everything that remained was trashed and broken. He closed his eyes and recalled trudging along such aisles during the weekly run for groceries, pushing a trolley through muddled ranks of shoppers while Tom talked about the latest *Doctor Who* episode.

Gus opened his eyes and aimed his torch upwards at the fluttering of bats hanging from the ceiling. Small eyes gleamed in the light. With darkness falling, some of them were already flapping about in shadowy corners and alcoves.

"Can we stay at the fire station tonight?" Tom asked. "It's just up the road."

"I don't see why not. Let's check it out."

Tom waved a goodbye to the bats.

They left the supermarket.

*

The fire station had suffered little damage during the outbreak and the following months. The front windows were intact but cloudy with grime, and a length of guttering pipe swayed in the breeze, hanging loose from its bracket. Gus led Tom up to the front of the building. The large roller doors were raised and the vehicle bays beyond were empty. The fire engines had never returned from their last call.

They stepped inside. Old ghosts of oil spillage stained the floor. Tom looked around with his mouth open and something like wonder in his eyes.

"I always wanted to visit a fire station," he said.

"I should have taken you to one before," replied Gus. "I'm sorry."

"It's okay, Dad." Tom walked over to the fireman's pole and looked up to the circular hole admitting it to the ground floor.

Gus stood beside him. "Shall we do some exploring before we settle in?"

Tom nodded. Gus led the way with the torch that Tom had given to him. Shadows retreated. Silence in the corridor and rooms beyond.

*

A gym room of dust-covered exercise bikes and cross-trainers. The kitchen was small and smelled of old bins. Gus went through the lockers in the changing room, but found nothing of use. Tom wore a discarded yellow helmet and fireman's jacket as he and Gus trudged about the deserted station.

Without electricity they had to close the roller doors by pulling the metal chains. By the time he was finished, Gus had to sit down and regain his breath.

After Tom slid down the pole a few times and wore himself out, they ate a dinner of Monster Munch and chocolate in the canteen. They sat at a table away from the darkened windows. Tom didn't take off his helmet or jacket, and Gus was happy to indulge him.

When it was time to go to sleep, they retreated to the accommodation area and pulled down two fold-out beds from the wall. Tom sat on his bed, slapping one hand upon the mattress. His eyelids drooped.

Soon afterwards they were both asleep and dreaming of the years before the blight.

CHAPTER SEVENTEEN

Gus woke upon the grass outside the fire station, on his knees and pawing at his chest with slick hands in the darkness. His breath came out as hot mist. He was shivering violently. He squeezed his eyes shut, hoping to quell the metallic ringing in his ears, and when it eventually faded he lowered his head and placed his hands on the damp grass.

A fluttering sound in the sky caused him to raise his head. He looked up at the dark. Shimmering stars glimpsed beyond patchy clouds. He thought about the bats in the supermarket. Then he wondered if he was mad and the only bats were in his belfry.

When the small, black shapes emerged into view, diving towards him, he realised that they weren't bats but birds, falling towards him with their sharp beaks and eyes gleaming darkly.

Crows.

They filled the sky and poured towards him.

*

He screamed as the crows swarmed about him, pecking at his flailing arms with their beaks. Their cawing and screeching cries were like the sound of nightmares.

Tom stepped onto the grass and raised his arms. Yellowish light bloomed in his hands as he stood beyond the wall of swooping crows. And then the jaundiced light, the light of disease, flared and swept the crows from the sky.

Great shrieks and human-like wails filled the air, and Gus covered his ears with his hands as he trembled into a foetal shape on the grass. He flinched as feathered bodies hit the ground around him. Then Tom was crouching beside him, groping for his hand. Gus held out his hand for Tom to take and the boy pulled him to his feet and they staggered towards the front door of the fire station.

A voice behind them made them halt and turn around.

"*Greetings, my friends!*"

A crumpled figure, no taller than a child, coalesced out of the dark. But it wasn't a child, not with such grey hair and withered features. Its squirming body bulged within a stained school blazer and maroon shorts. Bloated stomach and thin arms. Buckled shoes and bandages.

"Who the fuck is that?" said Gus, his shoulders sagging. He grimaced at the small cuts inflicted by the crows' beaks.

Tom squinted at the figure, who regarded them with a knowing smile and a small nod of its blackened head. Then Tom's eyes widened, as if he'd happened upon a startling piece of knowledge.

"His name is John Smith. That's the name he gave himself. He's powerful."

And as they watched John Smith, his eyes glowed with yellowish light and he began to drift towards them on legs that didn't move.

Gus and Tom stumbled inside and slammed the door.

*

They retreated onto the vehicle bays, and before they could turn to flee down the corridor, the front door was smashed open and John Smith stepped inside, grinning madly, a funhouse horror in a schoolboy's outfit.

The crows swarmed through the open doorway, past John Smith. Gus dragged Tom down a corridor as the crows flocked and bustled. Tom slipped free of his father's hands and turned to face the birds. Gus shouted to him. Tom held out his hands and they glowed with the yellow light, and the light grew and bloomed and turned the air as hot as an oven.

Tom screamed as the light filled the corridor and burned the crows to ashes. And when the light faded and the smouldering remains of the crows smoked on the floor, John Smith appeared, the manic grin still plastered on his blackened and weeping face. He burst into a fit of giggles.

"Well, that's unfortunate."

"Go away," Tom said.

John Smith's eyes glowed fiercely. "I don't think so, young one. It's time for this messing about to stop. You have to remember who you are. You have to come with us, youngling." With that he banged his fists on the walls and thin fractures ran the length of the walls all the way to where Tom stood.

Tom recoiled, backing into Gus, and they fell against the closed door behind them. The boy was breathing hard. He looked feverish and dazed. Using his capabilities seemed to drain him.

John Smith started towards them, floating above the floor.

Tom straightened and stood in front of Gus, shielding his father. He held up one hand, palm facing outwards, and John Smith halted, frozen in place. The grin died on his mouth. He snarled, and his teeth were all brown and swimming in blood.

Tom's shoulders were juddering and shaking. He bowed his head. The air seemed to curdle. A thin trail of blood seeped from Tom's left ear.

Gus didn't realise what the ripping sound was until he looked up and saw the corners of John Smith's mouth widening into a bloody smile. The short man made a muffled cry as the flesh of his cheeks split to accommodate the spreading grin. He pawed at his face as blood gushed from the growing wound and spilled over his lower lip and chin. Soon he was vomiting blood onto the front of his blazer, and his terrible smile widened to split his face into two rubbery pieces. He raised his face to the ceiling, gagging and choking as blood filled his throat. His mouth stretched open obscenely, like that of a boa constrictor, and he was trembling all over, caught in a fit of convulsions.

"End it, Tom," Gus said. "Do it."

Tom screamed.

John Smith's upper jaw unhinged, the mandibles snapping, and the top half of his head tore free as though it was pulled by invisible hands. It flopped wetly to the floor, eyes glazed and dull, followed by the rest of the body.

The broken remains steamed among the ashes of crows.

"Holy fuck," Gus said. "Holy fucking shit…" He barely caught Tom before the boy hit the ground. Tom's eyes were open, and Gus thought the he was dead until a check of his pulse found a faint beat.

Laughter rang out from the front of the building. More Nephilim had arrived.

Gus dragged his son from the corridor.

CHAPTER EIGHTEEN

They fled into silvery darkness. Gus half-carried his son through the blight-infected woods outside the town, stumbling between thin trees as blackened branches and limbs scratched, slapped and flailed at them. His limbs and shoulders ached. He breathed through gritted teeth. The cold air found his wounds and sent sharp bolts of pain into his body.

The Nephilim called to them in the distance. Distorted voices, cruel laughter and keening cries. Gus imagined them creeping through the woods, closing on him and Tom.

The boy was unresponsive, struck dumb, as if something had failed inside him. Gus would deal with it later.

Far behind them, beyond the trees, the Nephilim called their names.

"Stay with me," Gus said to his boy. "We'll be okay."

The wind ghosted through the treetops. The moon waned, losing to the darkness. Gus glanced about in a panic, seeing faces and shapes that weren't there. He struggled to keep a lid on his terror. He thought he could hear crows flying over the woods, waiting to attack again.

He almost laughed. He was sick of crows.

*

They staggered onwards through brush and thickets, and Gus looked back and saw bright-eyed figures moving between the trees, edging closer, laughing and having a whale of a time.

"Oh shit," he muttered.

The Nephilim's glowing eyes turned towards his voice.

"Let me go," Tom whispered.

"No." Gus dragged his son over a moss-covered tree stump and through a squabble of branches. "I'm not leaving you again."

"You have to let me go, Dad. They're going to catch us. I can fight them."

"I can fight them too."

"Not like I can, Dad." Tom slipped from his father's hands and fell down. He rose as Gus turned to grab him again, but his hands were glowing with the yellow light, forcing Gus to back away.

"You have to go, Dad."

Back in the trees, the Nephilim cackled and whooped. Their voices entwined in a cacophony of insults and gleeful threats.

"I'm not leaving you," Gus said.

"Okay," muttered Tom. "Okay. If that's the way it's gonna be." The boy raised one hand and the yellow light within it flared and sent Gus flying backwards like he'd been hit by a car. The sky and the earth swapped places and the trees batted him about like he was a lump of wet rags. He hit the damp ground and rolled into a ditch, gasping for breath, his lungs empty and drained.

After pulling some air into his chest, he crawled to the lip of the ditch and saw Tom disappear into the darkness towards the Nephilim. He called out for Tom, told him to come back, but he could only shout for a few seconds before his voice failed him and he collapsed onto his chest.

There was a scream off in the trees. Gus lifted his face from the dirt and dead leaves. Brief pulses of light flashed beyond the ditch, followed by the sound of trees being ripped from the earth. A shriek rose from the dark.

Gus watched as the woods before him erupted into flame.

CHAPTER NINETEEN

A *beach. The past. A memory of a sunny day in winter. Waves breaking upon the shore of sand and gritty pebbles. Gulls cry above the dark sea.*

Tom runs along the water's edge, hollering and laughing, kicking his wellies through the thinnest part of the shallows while Gus and Freya watch from the beach. He runs to them, a staggering tangle of limbs in his yellow coat, and they gather him up like a bundle of sticks. Such a slight boy, but one filled with wonder and happiness. He is the brightest thing in their life; a manifestation of their years together.

Tom hugs them both and complains that he has wet feet, but there is joy in his voice and the smile never leaves his face.

*

G us came to sucking at the warm air and scraping at the dirt with his shaking hands. Bright sunlight stung his eyes. His mouth and the inside of his throat felt like he'd been inhaling toxic fumes. His head spun as he hauled himself from the ditch, desperate for water, muttering his son's name. The wounds inflicted by the crows stung and itched.

All around him the trees were charred and ashen, flash-burned and black. The fire had consumed the heart of the wood. Embers and charcoal crackled under his feet as he walked back to where Tom had disappeared into the dark. The ground was still warm. Ash twirled and drifted in the air, which tasted of wood smoke and burnt vegetation. Each breath scraped at his lungs. Something inside his chest felt raw and tender, as if he'd been coughing for hours without respite.

He found the first corpse, a curled up thing of taut and blackened skin stretched over assembled bones, grimacing at the state of itself.

It wasn't Tom.

There were several more bodies scattered about. Little more than bones in charred rags that flapped in the breeze. Scalps with the hair burnt away. Empty eye sockets and grinning mouths. He studied each corpse until he could look at them no longer. His son wasn't among them.

"Where are you, Tom?" he whispered.

No answer from the scorched earth, just the sigh of ash falling about him.

*

Gus emerged from the ruined woods and found a burned man crawling along the road. He pulled the lock knife from his pocket. The man glanced back, and his horribly charred face slackened in surprise when he saw Gus. He tried to crawl faster, but all it did was scrape his skin over the road and leave bits of himself in his wake.

Gus stepped into the road and followed the trail until he caught up with the man and pressed his foot down on his back. The man exhaled sharply as his face hit the tarmac.

"You're one of them, aren't you?" Gus said.

The man's voice was muffled and wet. "Who's 'them'?"

"The Nephilim."

The man grunted. "Your boy's dead."

Gus's breath caught in his chest. "You're lying."

"I saw him die."

"That's a lie."

"Why would I lie to you?"

"Because you're a piece of shit, like your friends. Where is he?"

"He's dead and gone, you prick. All burned up. Died crying for his daddy, wailing like a bitch. I thought you should know that." And then the man was laughing as he spluttered spit and blood from his mouth. His laughter shrilled inside Gus's head.

Gus bit down on his lip until he tasted fresh blood. Tears welled in his eyes as his shoulders started trembling and he bunched his hands into whitened fists.

The man kept laughing.

Gus crouched next to the man's head and grabbed a handful of his scorched hair and pulled so that one side of his face remained stuck to the tarmac like some melted half-mask. His cackling grew louder, hysterical, blood and lymph pouring from his face. His lunatic eyes widened. The grin on his ruined face turned Gus's anger into white-hot rage.

The man kept laughing.

Gus didn't think; all he could see was Tom's face in his mind. He screamed and thrashed, and he smashed the man's head against the road over and over again until the laughter stopped and the front of the man's skull was caved-in like a broken egg. And when he finished, he looked at the man's head in his bloodied hands and let out a small whimper, his eyes streaming tears.

He released the man's head and let it drop back onto the road, then stood and backed away from the body, wiping his hands on the thighs of his jeans. Then he turned away and started up the road, with pained thoughts of Tom in his mind.

CHAPTER TWENTY

Judging from the sun's place in the sky, Gus reckoned it was close to midday. He'd passed through more silent villages, watching the road, watching the heavens, huddled against the cold as he dragged his exhausted body along the tarmac. The wind rippled over fields of long grass and gone-to-seed crops.

There was pain in every movement and step. He imagined Tom was walking with him, urging him softly to keep going. He smiled at the thought; he would keep going until his legs gave way and he collapsed into a heap of bones.

Just outside the village of Milborne Port, he came across a pack of crows feeding on a corpse. When he stepped closer, careful of the birds, he saw it was a woman. The crows must have just started on her before he arrived, because she was mostly intact and the soft parts of her still remained.

Gus stopped, put one hand around the knife in his pocket. The crows swivelled their heads and appraised him coldly. Blood dripped from black beaks. They were spread over and around her, perching on her arms and legs, staking their claim for the carrion. One crow had alighted on the back of her neck and dipped its head to peck at the saggy skin there. The woman's face was all shrivelled black and agape, her eyes still open and livid in the agony in which she'd died. The shawl over her shoulders flapped in the breeze. Her fur coat, most of which was scorched by fire, had fallen down her back, exposing the blackened skin over her hunched spine. Her tracksuit bottoms were charred and torn, as was the skin of her legs. Gus pictured her stumbling from the woods after the fire, badly wounded and gasping, following the road until she collapsed here.

He walked around the crows and their feast. The birds watched him leave. They had no interest in him when there was meat already available.

*

His boy's apparition stayed with him on the long walk, and he was grateful for the conversation. Tom told him to keep going. Tom told him to keep his eyes on the road. Tom told him to walk the winding path and never look back.

Gus nodded as he listened, arms folded, head down, his boots scuffing on gravel, dead leaves and ash.

"Where am I going, Tom?"

Tom didn't answer, because he was dead, and Gus was alone in the wasteland.

Gus wiped his eyes as he mumbled an old song that Tom liked when he was very young. Gus didn't know the words, but that didn't matter.

Hours passed in grim daylight. The blight was prospering and growing, strangling the land in its black tendrils. It was a terrifying sight to see fields, hedgerows and trees slowly being consumed. His heart winced and ached.

Rain fell in brief showers that soaked him and tested his resolve. Gus spoke still to his boy and shared a joke upon the long stretches of road. He imagined his boy laughing, and it brought him to tears again.

The pain in his legs forced him to rest, and he sat on the bench in a sheltered bus stop. He eased his legs out and straightened them, exhaled deeply and closed his eyes.

Time passed in the slow ticking of his heart. He thought of Freya and the years before her death, and how she would laugh while trying to tell a joke, and end up ruining the punchline. But he would laugh anyway, just to make her feel better.

She'd been gone for a while. His last memory of his wife, after the cancer had wasted her to a skeletal effigy of her old self, was of the final hours spent sitting beside her bed as he waited for the hospital staff to take her down to the morgue.

When he opened his eyes he saw a thousand-strong flock of black butterflies writhing above the field across the road.

They were from the blight, born from the disease, but they were beautiful.

And after a while, the butterflies flocked out of sight behind dark thickets and the fields beyond the road, so Gus rose to his feet and started walking again.

CHAPTER TWENTY-ONE

He reached the village of Sherborne in the last hour of daylight, and entered a house set back from the side of the main road. He checked the rooms. All deserted. He didn't stop to examine the trinkets and belongings of the former occupants. No point in looking into other people's memories.

Gus slumped on the sofa and laid his head back and stared at the ceiling with eyes stinging from the salt in his sweat. His heartbeat was the only sound. He slipped his boots off and drank from the dusty can of Lilt he'd liberated from the back of the kitchen cupboard. It was flat, but delicious and soothing down his throat. Then he sank into the padded embrace of the sofa, and to distract his mind from the wracking aches in his body he thought of good times with his wife and Tom.

He stayed like that for a long while, weeping softly for his lost boy.

*

During the night he ate the small amount of stale food he'd scavenged from the house and finally slipped into a sleep of nightmares and flashing lights. Softer dreams followed, of the plaintive songs of black stars and dying constellations, and he saw the vast abyss of the cosmos, but it terrified and haunted him and he woke babbling into his clammy hands.

Pale light edged through the window.

A man in an old fashioned trench coat was standing in the corner of the room. His face was blackened and seeping, a watchful horror with grey teeth.

Gus opened his mouth but found he couldn't speak as the Nephilim creature stepped towards him.

"I'm not going to hurt you," the man said, halting after one step. Thin, reedy voice. Apologetic and wan. He was terribly thin, but tall enough to tower over Gus.

Gus rose from the sofa with his knife already in hand, but before he could lunge towards the man there was a shrill ringing inside his skull and he collapsed onto one knee, clasping the sides of his head. It felt like glass shards in his brain, and he cried out and dropped the knife.

Then the pain and the ringing stopped, and Gus knelt there gasping and shaking.

"I don't want to hurt you," the man said.

Gus snatched the knife from the floor and tried to stand and move towards the man, but when the ringing returned to his mind and the pain scraped in his ears, he fell back down and lay on his back as his limbs convulsed and his hands curled into palsied claws against his stomach.

The man loomed over Gus and bent down to take the knife. He put it in his pocket then crouched beside Gus, his blackened face morose and weeping. The yellow light left his eyes and they returned to their normal shade of blue. He put one cold hand over Gus's hands. Gus stilled and the convulsions faded from his arms and legs. The ringing abated, as did the pain.

The man seemed to attempt a half-smile, but upon his ruined face it was merely a thing of horror.

Gus looked up at the man, breathing hard as he tried to pull air back into his lungs. He couldn't move.

"It's okay," the man said. "If I wanted to kill you, I would have already done it."

"What do you want?" Gus muttered.

"I want to help you."

"Why?"

"Because you think your son is dead. But he's not dead. And I have a score to settle with the Nephilim."

CHAPTER TWENTY-TWO

His name was Nolan and he was an outcast. He kept scratching at his face and glancing around at the shadows. He smelled of compost heaps and fermentation. Gus kept one hand on the knife Nolan had returned to him.

"The man you killed," Nolan said as he helped Gus back onto the sofa. "He lied to you about your son."

Gus looked at him. "What?"

"Your son isn't dead. The Nephilim are taking him to the place where the black rocks fell."

"Why should I believe you?"

"Because it's the truth."

"How do I know it's the truth?"

"Because I could have killed you any time I wanted, and I'm trying to help you."

Gus swallowed a sore lump in his throat. "Have you been following me?"

Nolan nodded. "I've been following you since you killed the injured man. Good job with bashing his head in, by the way. Before that, I was tracking the Nephilim. I'm still tracking them, but they're far ahead of us."

"What are they going to do with my boy?"

"The truth may upset you," Nolan said.

"It's all a bit late for that. Tell me."

Nolan scratched around his mouth. "Your son is not who you think he is."

"What the hell does that mean?"

"He's the Gelding."

"My son is the leader of the Nephilim? Are you serious?"

"Did he mention the Gelding?" said Nolan.

"Tom said that the Gelding was the worst of them all." Gus shook his head. "How is Tom supposed to be the Gelding?"

Nolan rubbed his eyes with gnarled hands. His nails were ragged and filthy. "Tom was leading a hunting party through the upper floor of an abandoned house; they were chasing an old man who'd somehow survived for months. Tom fell through a patch of rotten floorboards and into the room below; hurt himself pretty bad. He was out cold for days. Then he woke and something had changed, and whatever it was healed his skin and returned Tom's original personality. But he still had his capabilities."

"And what happened then?" said Gus.

"Tom fled into Salisbury and hid from the Nephilim."

"Tom told me he'd had amnesia for the last six months. He only remembered hiding from the Nephilim in Salisbury."

"He can't remember being the Gelding."

"How long ago did this happen?"

"A few weeks ago."

"That's when I first started to get the dreams," Gus said. "When he started to reach out to me."

"Did he tell you about the god inside of him?" said Nolan.

"Tom said the Nephilim want the god for their own uses, and they want to rip it out of his body."

"That's true," Nolan said. "The god has been gestating for months, but it's nearing the time for its birth. When Tom was the Gelding he planned to take the god to the place where the black rocks had fallen. I'm guessing you and Tom were heading to the impact site when the Nephilim caught up with you."

"I can't believe this," said Gus. "It's not possible."

Nolan shrugged. "Anything's possible now. Things have changed. I have no reason to lie to you."

Gus eyed the thin man. "I can't trust you."

"But you believe me, don't you?"

"I don't know. But I have to get Tom back from those fuckers. If he's still alive."

Nolan nodded. "Fair enough." He picked a scrap of blackened skin from his neck and appraised it, then flicked it away. "Shall we get going? We've still got a way to go."

Gus looked at the floor. Thoughts swirled in his mind and left him confused, but there was renewed hope inside him, and it was both cruel and wonderful.

He raised his face towards Nolan, but the man was already walking out of the room.

CHAPTER TWENTY-THREE

They walked the road, negotiating broken tree branches and abandoned vehicles. Gus kept his distance from Nolan. Glimpses of sunlight flared in the ashen sky.

"You want to know why I'm not with the Nephilim, don't you?" Nolan said without looking at Gus.

Gus stared down the road, flexing one hand around the knife in his pocket. "You can tell?"

Nolan grunted, chewed on his fingernail. "I don't need my capabilities to know that."

"You're very perceptive."

Nolan laughed, but it wasn't a nice sound.

"Aren't you gonna tell me then?"

The thin man cleared his throat and grimaced. "I couldn't kill people anymore. I couldn't hurt people anymore. Something changed inside me. I don't know how or why it happened. Thing is, the Nephilim don't like that sort of attitude, so they banished me. But not before they tortured and beat the shit out of me as example to any others considering a change in lifestyle. Then they left me for dead. Unfortunately for them, I recovered. Mostly."

"You want revenge?"

"Yeah. And to help you and your son."

"Why help us? We haven't done anything for you."

Nolan frowned at the dismal light. "The Nephilim want to leave the quarantine zone, conquer Great Britain and make the 'normals' their slaves. They think they're better, more evolved. I can't let that happen."

"You grew a conscience," said Gus. "Impressive."

"Not really. It was always there, but the blight was stronger. Then I realised I couldn't be a monster anymore. Maybe my humanity grew back, I don't know."

Gus looked at him. "So, you don't feed on people?"

"Not for a while, now."

"How do you survive?"

"Rats, birds, small mammals. Even insects, if I'm really desperate. It's better than nothing. I drain them of their life, their spark. I haven't eaten normal food since before I was infected."

"Are you not tempted to feed on people again?"

Nolan hesitated, wiped his mouth. "All the time. Although there aren't many normal people left in the Quarantine Zone. The Nephilim caught most of them. That's another reason they want to break out of the Zone – they need another food source – more people."

"I see," said Gus.

The thin man snorted. For no reason at all, he spat laughter from his damp mouth. "Anyway, let's talk about something else, shall we?"

"Okay."

"What's your favourite film?"

"The Big Lebowski."

"Yeah?"

"Yeah."

"Nice choice. Do you want to know mine?"

"No."

"Okay."

*

The road winding and rising through the countryside. Drizzle fell and stopped, then fell again, and it was always cold.

They arrived in Yeovil and walked the roads within the town. Crows circled in the sky. Gus wondered if the birds were waiting for them to collapse from exhaustion. Nolan said nothing as he appraised the blight-infected walls of buildings. Many of the trees and other vegetation were also stricken by the disease. The air smelled of rotting flowers.

Silence prevailed down the streets. Desolation and a sense of bittersweet loss, of grief and melancholy. Deserted shops and restaurants, pubs and offices. In a playing field was a towering pile of human remains, desiccated and blackened. A mangy dog loitered near the mound of corpses, licking its paws in the snatches of weak sunlight. It sniffed at the air and turned its head towards Gus and Nolan, staring at them until they moved out of sight.

Flecks of ash on the breeze scratched at Gus's face. He spat, wiped his eyes. Nolan frowned at the sky.

They reached the town centre. Gus slumped on a bench to rest. He felt listless and wrung out. It was a struggle to fill his lungs. His pulse banged and scraped in his ears, and his legs were covered in jabbing aches. His injuries from the crows' attack were constant pain. He put one hand to the small of his back and winced.

Nolan caught a rat and drained the life from it with his hands. Gus turned his eyes away and tried not to listen to Nolan's low grunts and gasps as the man ingested the precious life-force.

When Nolan was finished, he placed the dead rat on the ground. His mouth was trembling and his eyes gleamed wetly. He leaned against the wall of a burnt-out grocery store, face lowered towards the ground, muttering to himself.

Because Gus was watching the thin man, he didn't see the woman step from the doorway across the road until she cleared her throat. And as he turned towards the woman, she raised her shotgun, and Gus saw her eyes above the barrels and his heart almost stopped.

CHAPTER TWENTY-FOUR

"Who are you?" the woman said. From behind her emerged several men with baseball bats, hammers, crowbars, and clenched fists. They spread out behind her, like a street gang fixing for a scrap.

Nolan backed up against the wall with his hands held out, as if he was gently holding back an invisible assailant.

Before Gus could answer, the oldest of the men nodded at Nolan and said, "He's one of the freaks. Look at his skin. He's infected."

"I can see that, Geoff," the woman said.

"I'm just saying…"

"Shut up, Geoff, for fuck's sake."

Geoff shut up.

Gus rose from the bench and kept his hands visible, glancing at the shotgun. The woman stiffened, narrowed her eyes at him.

"He's not one of them," Gus said. "He doesn't kill people."

The woman looked at Nolan. "Get away from the wall and stand next to your friend here."

Nolan did as he was told. He stood beside Gus and put his hands on his head.

The woman and the men stepped towards them. The man called Geoff breathed with his mouth open and kept clenching and unclenching his fingers around the grip of his baseball bat. His brow glistened with sweat. His eyes never left Nolan. He looked terrified and angry.

Gus looked at him. "Easy there, mate."

"Piss off," Geoff sneered as he glanced at Gus. "You're the one hanging around with a freak."

"Let's all just calm down," Nolan said.

One of the other men jerked his head forward in anger. "Don't tell us what to do, you fuckin' freak."

The woman batted her hand at the younger man. "You can shut up, too, Wayne."

Wayne frowned, his face reddening. He didn't reply. He and two other men walked around Gus and Nolan and stood behind them.

The woman looked at Gus. "You, on the other hand, better start talking."

Gus swallowed. "We're just passing through."

"What're you doing hanging around with his kind? Surprised he hasn't drained you by now. You'd make a nice meal for him, I reckon."

"I'm not like the others," Nolan said.

"In what way?"

"I don't kill people. I don't hurt people."

Geoff snorted, wiped his nose with the sleeve of his dirty coat. "Sounds like bollocks, June."

"Is it bollocks?" the woman asked Gus.

"It's not bollocks," he said. "That's the truth."

The men behind Gus laughed without humour. Gus cringed, tensing for the impact of bludgeons against his back.

"I'm Gus," he said. "This is my companion Nolan."

"Companion?" said Geoff, frowning. "You a pair of fags? You bummers?"

Nolan almost laughed, but seemed to think better of it.

"I told you to shut up, Geoff," June said.

"I'm looking for my son," said Gus. "He was taken by the Nephilim."

"Who?" June said.

"The freaks," said Nolan. "They call themselves the Nephilim."

Geoff spat and jabbed a finger at Nolan. "You're one of them. Piece of shit. Motherfucker."

Nolan said nothing and looked at the ground.

"He's helping me find my son," said Gus.

"I find that hard to believe," June said. "And you wouldn't believe that either if you've seen what they've done."

Geoff wrinkled his nose like he'd smelled something bad. "Yeah, fuckin' right. The bastards killed my family. Drained the life outta them."

"They killed my wife," another man said, his eyes wild with adrenaline as he tapped his finger on the end of a metal pipe.

"They killed my son," the man next to him spat. "I saw it happen. They're monsters."

"They're evil!" another man said.

Nolan looked around at the men. He kept wiping around his mouth and down his chin.

"I don't kill people. I don't kill people. I don't…"

June narrowed her eyes at Nolan. "If you don't kill people, what do you feed on then? Fresh air?"

Nolan told her.

Some of the men laughed dismally, their faces full of disbelief and florid with anger. Gus felt their belligerence hustling around him, like heat trembling in the air. Their voices grew louder, bristling with rage and injustice, and grief for their lost loved ones. Their blood was up and they wanted to release their anger through violence. Gus had seen it outside nightclubs and football grounds. They were building up to something. It was like a temperature gauge rising steadily.

Gus wondered if they would kill him, too. Because they would kill Nolan, he was sure.

The attack happened fast.

One of the men, who before had only been a jittery and anguished face to Gus, rushed forward from behind the others and raised the length of rebar in his hands. Gus shouted something wordless. Nolan watched the man approach and did nothing.

The rebar fell quickly, the man grunting and wild-eyed as he brought it down with palsied hands. It was a clumsy attack and the man seemed unsure of his own conviction. The metal bar struck Nolan a glancing blow across his forehead. But it was enough to put him down on his knees with blood dribbling from his head.

The mob roared with approval. Shouts and spittle-flecked insults. Boots and trainers scraping on the tarmac.

Gus reached out to Nolan, but the woman clipped him on the side of the head with the shotgun butt and he fell down beside the other man, on his arse and dazed like a drunk. The world turned in all directions as he slumped onto his back. He put one hand to where he'd been struck, and felt some small relief that he wasn't bleeding. Then he looked over at Nolan, now cowering from the mob.

"Get stuck in, lads," June said. "Break him into bits." She turned and looked at Gus. Her face was deathly pale and tired, but there was a hint of a smile.

Gus tried to sit up, but his vision swayed drunkenly and his head was pounding, and all he could do was lie down and listen to the anger of the mob.

He noticed that the sky had cleared and was mostly blue.

"I'm sorry, Tom," Gus whispered.

Nolan screamed as the mob laid into him with fists, feet and makeshift weapons.

CHAPTER TWENTY-FIVE

Gus was still staring at the sky when the mob's angry sounds became screams of pain. A man stumbled past him and collapsed onto all fours, shaking his head like he was trying to cast out bad thoughts. Gus turned his head to one side to see the man, who was bleeding from the eyes, mouth and ears. The man's body was convulsing and steaming. A wet choking rasp spilled from between his lips in a surge of red froth, and he uttered a cry of sheer agony before he began vomiting blood.

Gus turned away and sat up. The men of the mob writhed and whimpered on the ground, curled into foetal shapes, crying and bleeding, hands withdrawn to cover faces and arms held close to bodies. June had dropped the shotgun when she'd collapsed, and she now lay on her back with blood trickling from the corners of her eyes. Her mouth was agape, lips wet with saliva. Geoff was nearby, lying on one side, gently scratching his face and smearing blood across his cheeks as he gibbered and pouted. His hands were like pale claws.

And within the sprawl of the stricken mob, Nolan sat cradling his left arm to his chest, rocking back and forth. He was bleeding from numerous cuts and wounds, and one side of his face was puffy and swollen. Gus stood and ambled over to him and he looked up and smiled sadly.

"I didn't want to do it," Nolan said, with tears in his eyes. His voice was barely heard above the moans and whimpers of the others. "They left me with no choice."

"I know," Gus said. He offered one hand to Nolan. "We should leave."

Nolan nodded as he took Gus's hand. "Yes, we should leave it all behind."

*

It took over an hour to get out of Yeovil. Parts of the town had been burnt to the ground. They hid from packs of wild dogs that stalked the silent windswept streets. When it was safe to emerge from their hiding places they did so slowly and with much pain.

Nolan kept muttering under his breath, saying he was sorry, and wiping his eyes with a blackened finger encrusted with dried blood and filth.

Gus said nothing.

The light was fading across the land, throwing shadows and imagined apparitions. The men were a pair of bedraggled forms shuffling along the road, holding up each other with trembling arms and shoulders strained to breaking point.

"How much farther?" said Gus. Words pushed past sore and dried lips.

Nolan looked up the road. "We're very close."

"It'll be dark when we get there."

"Good. They won't see us coming."

*

In the growing darkness they emerged from behind a thicket of trees and halted on the road, staring at the immense column of yellow light rising beyond the nearby hills and climbing into the night sky, where it stretched upwards without end.

"What is it?" said Gus.

Nolan breathed out, sagged against him. The smell from his mouth was like raw sewage. "I think we're too late. I'm sorry, Gus. I truly am."

CHAPTER TWENTY-SIX

They left the road and climbed a low hill, and when they reached the hilltop they looked down to the fields beyond, wincing from the glare of the light. It was like the brightest sunlight Gus had ever seen, without a filter, but there was a coldness radiating from it. The column had consumed almost an entire field and was pulsing slowly. He was aware of a low thrumming.

"Oh god," he said. "What am I seeing?"

Nolan didn't answer.

In the field below, like an army of oddly clothed pilgrims, hundreds of Nephilim gathered around the column of light, which was coming from within the ground out of a large crater. The light revealed the immediate landscape, scarred and pitted. Some of the craters and holes suggested a great depth inside their absolute darkness. The ground was infected and blackened with the blight.

The place where the black rocks had fallen.

"They're not moving," said Nolan.

Gus wiped his eyes. "What?"

"The Nephilim aren't moving. Look at them."

Gus dragged his eyes from the pulsing light and looked carefully at the crowd: an army of scarecrows in charity shop fashions. And many of them had their heads bowed; inactive, like they were dormant or under a spell.

"It's incredible," said Nolan.

Gus nodded. "I'm going down there."

*

He left Nolan on the hilltop and went down to the field and stood at the edge of the crowd. Pain throbbed in his legs. The ground was sodden and stank like marsh water. The reek of the motionless bodies pinched at his eyes and curdled the bile in his gut. He looked at the Nephilim; frozen in their hunched forms, staring at the ground or the great column of light. The yellow light painted their faces with cruel demeanours and sly grins, revealing funeral suits and summer dresses, bowler hats and stained bonnets. Raggedy figures in peculiar clothes. Appalling shadows with long fingers.

Gus waited, hesitant to enter the crowd, his heart fluttering. He swallowed. Then he stepped into the mass of bodies, all the while expecting them to jerk awake like manipulated puppets and reach for him. But they remained unmoving. He moved carefully, afraid to touch them, keeping his arms to his sides as if he were moving through a tangle of poisonous vegetation. Sweat dripped into his eyes. He breathed lowly, sick with revulsion at the closeness of crooked limbs and leering faces. His eyes flicked over the motionless figures. He passed a man whose face was raised to the sky and frozen with a toothless grin. Glazed unseeing eyes visible through a fringe of greasy hair.

Some of the Nephilim were children. He saw the twin girls who'd attacked him in Salisbury; they were holding hands and smiling up at the light. He waved one hand before their faces, but they didn't react.

As he went on, searching for Tom amongst the forest of upright bodies, he became aware of a metallic ringing. The air buzzed with static and his skin tingled with gooseflesh. He neared the column of light and turned his head away from the near-blinding glare, stumbling on leaden feet. The ringing grew until it filled his head, but within it he could hear the voice of his boy calling to him. And he raised his face from his chest and looked into the light and thought he saw a vague apparition of Tom waiting for him. He halted.

"Tom," he whispered. "Is that you?"

The column of light pulsed, like a beating heart in a glass bell. Tom's phantom beckoned to him.

Eyes streaming tears, Gus smiled, and walked towards the light.

CHAPTER TWENTY-SEVEN

Past the light and into the darkness, Gus collapsed upon ground that wasn't the diseased dirt of the field. Sharp blades jangled inside his head. With his face pressed to the dust, he moaned at the pressure behind his stinging, watering eyes.

Footsteps approached in the dark. He looked up and wiped his eyes. A figure coalesced and stood before him.

"You came back for me," Tom said, smiling.

Then Gus passed out.

*

Flashes of light in the dark. Tom showed him images of alien worlds and starless desolation. Eternal darkness and eternal silence. Vivid glimpses of unknown constellations. The deepest reaches of the cosmos. Quasars and black holes, fading suns in the deep cold. The silent void.

The boy held Gus's hand and showed him a world covered with writing black, and he realised it was the planet where the blight was born. A world of primordial gods pulsing in black seas.

"This was the origin," Tom said, his voice serene. His hand was clammy and hot. He sounded different than Gus remembered.

"What about the god inside you?" said Gus.

Tom looked at him. "I am the god. The god is me."

"What does that mean?"

"Symbiosis," said Tom. "The Nephilim were wrong about the god; they couldn't cut it out of me. That's not the way it's supposed to happen."

"I don't understand."

Tom stared into the writing darkness. "You'll understand soon."

"What's happened to the Nephilim?" said Gus. "I had to walk through them to get to you. They didn't attack me."

A brief smile played across Tom's mouth. "I control them. They do the god's bidding. The god convinced me of its plans for this world. Convinced me to help spread

162

the blight. To make this world pure. A new paradise."

Gus looked at the boy. He resisted the urge to slip his hand free from Tom's as he realised the boy beside him was no longer his son.

"It'll all be revealed," said Tom.

"Don't do it," Gus said. "Don't listen to the thing inside you. The blight will kill millions."

"Do not be worried," Tom said. "It's for the best. It's all for the best."

"No, Tom."

The boy merely grinned, and around them the darkness bustled and roared with swarms of black butterflies.

Gus stepped back and let go of Tom's hand.

The boy's face creased with disappointment.

The black butterflies flocked in their endless numbers and the flitting of their wings filled Gus's mind. The insects emitted a buzzing sound that distorted the screams rising from the darkness. He dropped to one knee, holding the sides of his skull, beseeching Tom with his wide eyes and terrified mouth.

Shaking his head, Tom went to Gus and laid his hands on his father's shoulders. Gus looked up at the boy.

"It'll be okay," said Tom. "Everything will be fine."

Gus was trembling, nodding slowly.

Tom embraced him and there was only the darkness and the beating of a billion butterflies' wings

CHAPTER TWENTY-EIGHT

Gus woke gasping, shivering in the cold air of the night, sprawled upon sodden ground. Tom was crouching over him, smiling down with a benign expression. Beyond him the sky was full of stars.

"Where are we?" said Gus. He raised himself onto his elbows and glanced around, noticing that they weren't at the impact site anymore. "How did we get here?"

The smile didn't leave Tom's face. His eyes gleamed. "The god has many powers – it brought us here. All of us. There is work to be done."

"You're going to kill people," said Gus.

Tom wiped his mouth, and he stopped smiling. "Come with us. Be part of the new order."

"The new order? You're insane, Tom."

"Far from it," the boy said. "This is the only way."

"I won't be a part of it," said Gus.

"You already are," Tom replied.

"Please don't do this, Tom."

"It has to be done." And the boy walked past him, left him behind. Gus climbed to his feet and turned around as Tom went to join the hundreds of Nephilim walking towards the high wall that separated the Quarantine Zone from the rest of the country.

"Oh god," he whispered.

The wall was no less than fifty feet in height, running across the mainland. Soldiers lined the top of the wall, aiming rifles at the approaching Nephilim. Searchlights swept over the swarm of absurdly-clothed figures.

"HALT!" a voice announced from atop the wall. *"HALT OR WE WILL OPEN FIRE!"*

And the Nephilim did halt. Some of them were giggling to themselves or exchanging mirthful expressions with those beside them. Grins splayed upon blackened faces of scarred skin. They looked up at the top of the wall. A few of them muttered and tittered, holding hands to their faces. One of the Nephilim howled like a dog and then burst into a fit of hysterical laughter.

Gus raised one hand to shield his eyes from the searchlight. He was shivering so much that his teeth were chattering. He couldn't see Tom amongst the Nephilim.

And when the metallic ringing pierced the air, Gus put his hands to his ears. The Nephilim fell silent and lowered their heads. The ringing deepened into a low rumbling that seemed to rise out of the earth.

The ground began to shake, gentle at first, but then building into powerful tremors. Gus lost his footing and broke his fall with his hands. His arms took his weight. Sharp stones bit into his palms.

A sudden roaring. A crack appeared in the ground between the Nephilim and the wall, and widened and spread towards the wall and the soldiers lined upon it.

Gus stood and watched as the crack reached the wall. The wall shook and buckled, stone and mortar crumbling to fall to the ground. With a resounding crack and a deafening roar, a vertical split appeared in the wall, running from the ground to the summit.

The wall collapsed inwards.

Soldiers screamed and flailed as they fell in the cascade of rubble. Some were crushed by falling masonry; one man was impaled on a jagged length of rebar, and was still alive when the Nephilim started towards the great breach in the wall. Clouds of dust billowed.

The soldiers that remained on the wall opened fire.

CHAPTER TWENTY-NINE

Some of the Nephilim fell before they reached the breach. A mortar round landed in the midst of a cackling group and tore apart their bodies and sent severed limbs spinning into the air, leaving a smouldering crater in the ground. Screams and cries echoed through the smoke in the air. Brief glimpses of flame and flashes of light.

Gus watched as the Nephilim poured through the breach like an army of insects. The soldiers atop the wall directed their gunfire directly below them and into the breach, but it had little effect on the swarm. And then from beyond the wall came muffled detonations and juddering impacts.

Gus stepped over piles of rubble and broken bodies as he staggered into the breach and through to the other side of the wall, out of the Quarantine Zone. The air stank of hot metal and burnt flesh. When he arrived into the smoke and confusion of battle, he halted and stood staring at the chaos before him.

The Nephilim were slaughtering the soldiers.

Gus crouched low as stray bullets streaked through the air. A soldier who'd lost his rifle and helmet stumbled past Gus, holding his spilled intestines in his hands. Another soldier was on his knees and pawing at his face.

Gus stumbled onwards, past corpses and puddles of blood. He crouched and took a pistol from the hand of a dead soldier. Then he moved on, picking his way through the swirling smoke. The sound of a jet screaming overhead, and he ducked instinctively.

He saw a female Nephilim straddling a young soldier on the ground. She was staring at the man, using some kind of telekinesis to peel the skin from his face. Her hands stroked the stained shawl over her head. She tittered and sang nonsense. The soldier only stopped screaming when she placed one hand upon his shuddering chest and drained the life from his heart. And then she stumbled away from the dead man and laughed with her head raised to the sky.

A helicopter flew above and swept a searchlight over the ground. Gus cringed at a low explosion far ahead.

"Tom!" he cried, wiping his stinging eyes. He coughed the acrid, smoky air from his lungs. He walked and searched for his son as people died around him.

More Nephilim were torturing and killing soldiers, flaying and mutilating them. Rifles lay discarded on the muddy ground. Sporadic gunfire. The smell of burning oil. A soldier limped past, bleeding from his eyes, ears and mouth. Gus barely avoided colliding with him.

More bodies the deeper he went into the smoke. Ahead were burning buildings. Embers drifted in the air. A barracks was quickly being consumed by flames. The Nephilim pranced and capered before the fire.

"Tom!" he shouted, his voice hoarse, his throat raw.

A Nephilim ran into Gus and wheeled away giggling. It was a man in a brown suit and yellow shoes, his hands stained red. A glistening scrap of flesh dangled from between his long fingers. He blew a kiss to Gus and vanished into the smoke.

Far ahead, through the haze, Gus glimpsed soldiers retreating from the battleground. He stopped to think about that, but almost immediately started walking again, hands covering his mouth, his eyes streaming tears. He coughed until his chest was sore and his breath came in wheezing gasps.

Then he stopped.

A few yards ahead, a small form appeared out of the black-grey smoke.

Tom.

Gus reached for him. Tom turned around slowly, and there was blood on his face and he was grinning like a lunatic. His eyes were glowing with diseased yellow.

"Tom!" Gus was aware of the pistol in his hand.

The boy shook his head and began to back away. Gus followed until he slipped in a putrid mess of blood and mud and fell down.

Tom halted, looked down at him, still grinning.

Gus reached out with one hand, swallowing sour knots in his throat, biting his lip to stop the tears he wanted to cry for his lost son. "Stop this, Tom. Please."

As he started crawling towards his boy, pleading on his hands and knees, the first artillery shells whistled down and sent the world into roaring darkness.

*

Upon the ruined ground he rose to his knees and then stood and wavered drunkenly on the spot. He looked around. Bodies scattered over the ground in ragged piles and heaps. Pulped and blackened remains. He coughed at the reek of charred meat all about him.

The smoke had cleared from the area, but the buildings beyond were still burning, streaming fire into the dark sky. There was a road leading away, past groves of tall trees. Some of the trees were aflame, blazing like bonfire night celebrations.

A few Nephilim crawled or flailed uselessly on the ground, most of them mortally wounded and near death. The severed head of a man still retained the top hat upon it.

Gus searched for Tom, picking through shredded and broken bodies, until he found the boy lying under the sprawled corpse of an old woman wearing a leather apron and knee-length boots. Gus removed the old woman and crouched next to his son. Tom's body was intact, his eyes closed, and when Gus put one finger to the boy's neck he found a faint pulse. He could have cried with relief. He brushed dirt from the boy's face. Looked at the pistol in his trembling hand, and wondered if he had the strength to use it.

Damp footfalls approached slowly behind him and halted nearby. Gus turned around.

Nolan stood there, swaying on his feet. He looked dazed. His mouth was wet.

"You found him," Nolan said.

Gus nodded.

"He teleported all the Nephilim here. The god is more powerful than I ever thought." Then Nolan said, "I have to kill him."

"What?"

"I want revenge."

"I can't let you," said Gus, as he raised the pistol.

"You'll have to kill me," said Nolan. "Do you think you can do that?"

CHAPTER THIRTY

Gus pulled the trigger. Nothing happened.

He tried again and again until he finally gave up, and then he sagged and stepped back from Nolan.

"I guess it's my lucky day," said Nolan. He stared at Gus and bunched his hands into fists. Gus dropped the pistol as an immense pain bloomed inside his head, and he reeled away, clutching his face and crying lowly as he lost his footing and collapsed into a foetal shape.

Nolan stepped towards him, shoulders trembling, the chords bulging in his neck. His eyes were wide and pale yellow. "I don't want to do this, Gus. But you left me with no choice." He sounded almost apologetic.

Gus gripped the sides of his head; it felt like razor-winged insects were buzzing inside his skull. His spine arched and a clawed hand grasped his heart. The pressure behind his eyes forced them to bulge in their sockets. His mouth opened in a rictus of agony. He screamed. Blood poured from his nose and mouth.

"I'm sorry," Nolan said. Gus could barely hear him. "I truly am sorry."

Resigned to his last moments, Gus looked up at the man.

Nolan frowned. A moment of confusion upon his face. A small rivulet of blood ran from each eye. His mouth opened.

The agony left Gus's body, and he lay there gasping.

Nolan jerked as if he'd been struck by a stone. And then he clutched his stomach, and bent at the waist and vomited blood onto the ground. He went down on his knees with a wordless cry. Blood dribbled down his chin and onto his chest. He inhaled sharply and looked at his right hand.

Gus looked back at Tom, and saw the boy's body convulsing.

With his right hand, Nolan clawed at his own face, the fingernails scratching and raking at the blackened skin. He shrieked as the hand took hold of a flap of skin at his cheek and pulled violently.

Nolan screamed to the sky, peeling his own face. Gus watched, mesmerised by the horror. Nolan dropped the sopping mask of his face and went to work on his eyes, gouging at them with dirty fingers.

Behind Nolan, Tom sat up and turned towards the screaming man. His face held no emotion.

Nolan removed his eyes and held them in his palms and crushed them in his hands. His screams became shrill, beyond pain and terror, until Gus grabbed a rifle from the hands of a dead soldier and shot him several times.

Nolan went still and silent. The last breath out of his mouth was flecked with bloody spit.

Tom lay down and closed his eyes again.

Gus went to the boy and stood over him. His finger rested on the rifle's trigger. The barrel aimed at the boy's head.

"Tom," he whispered.

The boy didn't answer.

From somewhere in the distant sky, the sound of helicopter rotor blades slowly grew louder.

EPILOGUE

They fled back into the Quarantined Zone. Gus took Tom back to their old house in Salisbury and laid the boy in his bed and watched over him as rain fell in fierce storms.

He waited for the boy to wake up, every day with the rifle by his side. He scavenged food and water, slowly regaining his strength. But Tom only became weaker, and within weeks he was no more than a raggedy form of bones and skin. Yet, the boy clung to life, and while his heart still beat Gus did not lose hope.

*

Tom died in the last light of a rainy afternoon.

Gus wrapped the boy in a blanket and carried him out to the back garden. By torchlight he dug a grave and talked to his son and told him he was loved.

When the grave was deep enough, Gus lowered the boy into the ground and refilled the hole with loose earth. Then he patted down the dirt until it was even and stood at the graveside as the sky faded to full dark. He spoke words to the boy. Spoke of memories and dreams and things that could have been. And he said goodbye.

He looked up and saw the scratch of a distant meteor across the cold sky.

THE END

SLAUGHTER BEACH

BENEDICT J JONES

When glamour photographer William Marshall charters Dan
Curtis' boat *The Ariadne* for a photo-shoot on a remote tropical
island it's an offer too good to turn down. Beautiful scenery,
beautiful girls… what could possibly go wrong?

The island hides a deadly secret though and soon Don, the
photographers and models find themselves in a terrifying game of
cat and mouse with a deadly adversary where death lies in wait
behind every tree and boulder.

Slaughter Beach – where paradise becomes a blood-drenched hell.

DARK MINDS NOVELLA 1

WHAT THEY FIND IN
THE WOODS

GARY FRY

When Dr Matthew Cole supervises Chloe Linton's university research on a 16th Century warlock named Donald Deere, he is sceptical. Surely it's just a local legend intended to scare people. But as Chloe develops her research, Matthew becomes embroiled in sinister events. They are both drawn into the woodland where Donald Deere was supposed to reside. And what they find might tear apart their minds.

DARK MINDS NOVELLA 2

KIDS

PAUL M FEENEY

Matt and Julie head to her parents' big, remote house in the country, with their children Kayleigh, Carol and Robert, for a day out with friends and family. They intend spending the warm, summer's day doing nothing more strenuous than engaging in light, casual conversation, eating lunch and drinking tea, while the kids play in the background.

At least, that's the plan…

The kids disappear, only to return utterly, fundamentally changed. Something bad has happened to them, something *very* bad.

The day becomes a pitched battle between the adults and the violent psychopaths their children have become. How can the adults survive against such an enemy, how can they even fight back, when the very thing they have to fight against is their own flesh and blood?

DARK MINDS NOVELLA 3

Printed in Great Britain
by Amazon